FUTURE WITHOUT FUTURE

FUTURE
WITHOUT
FUTURE

JACQUES STERNBERG

A Continuum Book
THE SEABURY PRESS
NEW YORK

The Seabury Press
815 Second Avenue
New York, N.Y. 10017

English translation copyright © 1973 by The Seabury Press, Inc.
Designed by Carol Basen
Printed in the United States of America.

Original edition: *Futurs sans avenir,* © 1971 by Editions Robert Laffont,
  Paris
Translated by Frank Zero

LIBRARY OF CONGRESS CATALOGING IN PUBLICATION DATA

Sternberg, Jacques.
    Future without future.

    (A Continuum book)
    Translation of Futurs sans avenir.
    I. Title.
PZ4.S8395Fu3 [PQ2637.T386]   843′.9′14   73–6427
ISBN 0–8164–9170–4

Contents

FIN DE SIÈCLE

January 3, 1999

Take courage.

If the planet survives it, in less than twelve months it will finally enter the year 2000, which we've heard about for so long. And afterwards? I wonder if the fact of having arrived, somewhat winded, at a round figure, will call whatever it may be into question again. I doubt it. But zeroes, when there are several of them, are always impressive. No doubt this comes from writing checks.

January 5, 1999

I have had a triple window installed. The double window was not enough. Now, sleeping with my earplugs, I almost no longer hear the uproar of traffic. Luckily, I live on a relatively quiet street. If I lived fifty yards or so further down, I would have to do as all the famous hypersensitives do: wall up my windows, enclose myself in a cocoon of stone without skylights, in order to survive, to escape the perpetual uproar that inundates the city. Only a few years ago there was the blessing of a letup between midnight and 5 A.M. The reprieve has steadily dwindled, reduced now to a single short hour. To avoid hopeless traffic jams, a large number of drivers don't return until 3 A.M., and many job holders begin their stampede to their place of work on the stroke of four. I wonder what it will take before they house workers and employees *in situ*. It would eliminate a certain number of problems.

January 6, 1999

Among these problems, that of traffic jams is the one that is surest to rile me. It seems that it preoccupied the authorities as early as the 70's; now, they have taken no interest in it for at least fifteen years. They've given up on it. What can one do against absolute insanity, the apotheosis of delirium? It is only a few weeks ago that we got through the famous traffic jam of October 10, 1998, and that thanks only to the huge helicopter-cranes, that were able to carry the cars off in midair, to dump them in a single scrap heap in open country. But the traffic jam of November 26, 1998, has not been reabsorbed so easily. For several square miles, the cars formed one great jumble of steel that was starting to rust. They finally had to accept the necessity of blowing up all the houses in this befouled area. In a few weeks, this labyrinth of the center will be simply a deserted place, an enormous decay in the heart of the city. Then they will finally be able to extricate the cars. But everyone knows that this will cause hopeless stoppages in the adjoining streets, which are all very narrow. In the end, they will have to raze the entire city and make it a single highway with six hundred lanes. This is the one remaining solution, since the citizens refuse to abandon their cars. On the contrary, the day is coming when they will drive two cars at once, with one foot in each. And the third foot in the grave, as always. People will never learn anything. When one thinks that the government has just successfully launched the "Rush Hour" experiment, which allows every motorist to take full advantage of traffic jams, and that the response was total . . .

January 8, 1999

For a month now, I have been suffering almost constantly from migraine headaches. It's reached the point that, when people speak to me at the office, I have to remove my earplugs. Fortunately there's powdered aspirin in everything we eat. How we'd be suffering without that.

January 10, 1999

I wonder what the municipal representatives will propose for next year. This year, it is transparent cubes. Last year they exhibited cones, equally transparent. The representatives never come to disturb us before 3 A.M. or after 6 A.M. Fortunately, they are polite. They always apologize for having awakened us, and always in the same glacial manner. Disquieting when one thinks that the objects proposed never serve any purpose and, furthermore, are not for sale. If I had the audacity, I would gladly take the risk, and not open to the official service representative. Just to see. To wait and see. But audacity, here, has never worked for anyone. Especially for those who are solicited legally.

January 11, 1999

I was rather surprised to receive a packet by the first post. I never receive anything in the mail.

I opened it without haste or curiosity. It was a directory, accompanied by a circular and a rather high bill. The Bureau of Tariffs and Profits are launching a novelty on the market: a directory of nonsubscribers to domestic gas. I am in it. And the dues we have to pay are no lower than what they charge subscribers.

The authorities don't really know any longer what to

invent to get money out of us. Sometimes I wonder why no one has ever had the idea of making us pay interest on the ground we walk on.

January 12, 1999

I came back to my place at two in the morning, exhausted.

The Monthly Quiz Game, which has the entire city worked up, was held this time in the Bureau of Contracts where I work. And it was I who was chosen, with two other employees, to answer trick questions that apparently have to do only with the work, its corollaries, its substitutes and its metaphysics. Tedious and stupid questions, prepared with sadism by the Ministry of Leisure and the Office of Administration Culture. The interrogation took place in the great reception hall, and was conducted by three questioners in hoods covering their faces, and ten judges who decided whether the answers were to be accepted or rejected. Each unanswered question draws a penalty of fifty francs. At this rate, one loses everything quickly, all the more so as there is nothing really to win. No need to mention the penalty that an ironic or sarcastic answer would entail. No one in his senses would ever think of not taking these games seriously. Many of my answers were judged unacceptable; on several occasions I remained silent, but I only lost half of my salary. I've gotten off rather lightly. My two colleagues didn't come out so well. One lost his salary for two months of work, and the other imprudently failed to answer the question, "Why are you working here?" This was good not only for an official censure and a heavy fine, but the immediate transfer of his file to the Central Bureau of Indictment. A bad business! Generally, it's not far from indictment to imprisonment.

January 14, 1999

I have received a last notice from the Bureau of Domestic Air and Gas. I owe them five hundred francs for consumption of air during the last quarter. As for the gas, I never use it. I'm saving it for the day when I want to end it all. I'll have the satisfaction of knowing that, since I have no heirs, no one will be able to pay the Suicide Tax which the State will claim.

I will have to have my O.A.M. inspected—I refer to my Oxygenated Air Meter—since I think it's out of order. Five hundred francs of air in three months! But how can one do without it? Short of wearing a gas mask, like the poor. But that's so impractical. When one thinks that at one time one lived on the natural air! That kind of fooling around would get us to the morgue in a few hours. Ah well, the times are indeed ripe for a good airing out.

January 15, 1999

Over the radio, as usual, the Center for Distribution of Time has announced that, in order to save time, tomorrow will be canceled. Fortunately, I had nothing important to do on that day.

I didn't have anything important to do yesterday either. Nor on the day after tomorrow will I have anything important to do. I have not had, I do not have, I will never have anything important to do. Then why this week, this month, this year, this century?

At any rate, I decided to inquire at the Office of General Information, where I was greeted by the functionary with the apathetic courtesy that is required in offices.

"I'd like a suggestion," I told him.

They asked me to be more precise; my request seemed obscure.

"I would like to know what to do," I said finally.

"You are looking for work?"

"I refer simply to passing the time."

I was asked if I had the catalogue of home recreation; certainly, I said. I know it by heart. Odd jobs require a skill and materials which I do not possess. Social games are tiresome when one is playing them all alone, and are too complicated to simplify. No success has ever succeeded for me; neither have failures, or the work involved in telling lies; and roaming around Bureaupolis has always bored me.

"I was hoping for something more suggestive."

"For the moment, we do not see what we can do for you. Next year, perhaps . . ."

Next year, last year, everything is referred to the past or the future. To listen to them, one would think that surely no one ever lives in the present time.

January 17, 1999

As on every Saturday, I was visited by my lawful mistress, who came to earn her bread and butter, accompanied by our adoptive cousin. This obligation to form a family of no less than three persons is really one of the most absurd laws of our period. Especially when one has no children, and is obliged to adopt the first unknown brat that turns up. And all this to force you to make huge contributions to the Office of Household Supervision. As if what Sexual Allocations cost us was not enough for them.

The child hands me his family report for my signature, and my lawful mistress gives me her shopping bills. They scarcely look at me, no more than they think of me.

"How are you?" she asks me.

"Are you well?" he asks me.

"And you?" I say in my turn.

We learn, without joy or rancour, that we are fine. It has to go this way. Or one makes it go. At any rate, for better or worse, one goes on. It's more or less predetermined. Things are going well when nothing happens. When one dies, one goes away. And even when one is dead, one goes —to the graveyard.

They take their places, eat and then leave. In four years, I may ask for the divorce which I am entitled to every five years, but this will hardly get me anywhere. Liaison is obligatory here, whether with a legitimate woman or an illegitimate one that one sees once a month or once a week; so I may as well resign myself. It's been this way for a long time.

Fortunately, my weekly mistress returns in full the indifference I feel towards her, and prefers to live with her maternal guardians. She finds my apartment too small and too cluttered. It is true that in these two rooms there is such a labyrinth of boxes, shelves, and cases that I hardly see how I could put up a woman and child who do not strike me as particularly interesting collector's items. There is, of course, the third room where they might stay, but they don't know of its existence. I myself think only rarely of this empty room, which I have always kept boarded up, and which I call "the chamber." A chamber to what purpose, I have never known.

As it was never yellow with age, it cannot have held any mystery. I might have made it into a storeroom if only I had found something to throw away, I who save everything for eventual collections, even the ash of my cigarettes, even the dust I sweep up under my furniture. Or else, it might have been an office, if I had a knack for business.

To make matters short, not seeing how to utilize it, I

ended by having the room walled up, after the windows and door had been taken out. At least, in that way, it serves as a sort of insulator.

As things are, nowadays, a reserve of this kind will always be useful.

January 32, 1999

The year is beginning badly. The Center for Distribution of Time seems to be having some problems with the month of February. The temporal junctions at the end of the month have grown more and more difficult over the last few years. Time is wearing out, one might say. It seems to be flowing through the pipeworks with more and more difficulty. Invariably the center announces that February 1st is not available today. I suppose that, as sometimes happens, another parallel world has been using the same day at the same moment; and as the double employment of one space of time is strictly forbidden, the Center has had to resign itself to taking extraordinary measures. But not very spectacular. The first of February was never anything special—not even when it fell on Sunday; and this January 32nd was not much more striking. Not anything to file a complaint about at Temporal Reclamations. And nothing comparable to the scandal which erupted in 1997, when the Center officially canceled the week of Christmas, depriving us of four days off, and heartlessly going from December 23rd to January 1st, 1998. Even the *Quotidian*, the one newspaper that we're still allowed to read, made references to it, although it never criticizes anything, not even by insinuation.

Nevertheless, there must be something rotten in the state of time, because this substitute day has reached us in rather poor condition. The sound of passing time, as

offered to us by the Center has been more and more ob-
trusive the last few years, but today it was truly irksome,
almost intolerable. There are moments when one might
have taken it for the grating of a needle on a badly made
record. When one thinks of the exorbitant price that one
is obliged to pay for a week of citizen's hours, one may
well say that the Center could at least dispense with proving to its consumers that time is rapidly passing, and could
afford to grant an hour of respite, a minute of blessing.
The gloomy stutter of the pendulum was, all in all, more
reassuring. In the end, it evoked only the sound of a foot-
step, and not a sheer drop from one void to another.

February 3, 1999

My neighbor on the landing has just been condemned
to ten years in prison.

He has committed an extremely grave offense: in a fit of
rage, he ripped out the wires of the loudspeakers which
are installed in the walls of all apartments, and which
broadcast, twenty-four hours a day, the one program of
the State Radio, legally inflicted on us. No one can get out
of it, even if it's difficult to bear. Especially Wednesday,
which is the day for advertising and slogans. Still, you'd
think they would break up their slogans from time to time,
garnish them with a few bars of music. I think I still prefer Sunday, the day for political speeches, even if these
speeches have been the same since 1985. That's just it!
You finally stop hearing them!

February 4, 1999

When I arived at the office this morning, the men from
the Brigade of Religious Police were already there. These

are not the least dangerous of the police, and the dogs that accompany them are hardly reassuring, with their fangs shining with hate, and the steel crucifixes that swing beneath their jaws about as friendly as well-sharpened daggers.

"You!" one of the policemen said, as he thrust in my direction a steely finger, which also reminded me of a pocket crucifix.

I approached, already repentant, penitent, humble, and secretly terrified.

"You have faith, I suppose?" he asked me.

I nodded yes with my whole being, even if I didn't know exactly what faith might mean. On the other hand, I *do* know what it costs simply to be suspected of not having faith.

"The company priest has brought you to our attention. He has the impression that you follow rather absentmindedly at the ten o'clock mass."

Although I had agreed before, I now denied their charges with the same fervor. The daily mass has always seemed to me even more absurd than the daily work; but I also know with what hypocrisy one has to throw them off the scent, dissembling at every moment.

"It seems that you have not yet paid your Religious Allocations for 1998. How do you explain this delay?"

I tried to explain as well as I could, slightly uneasy as I saw that the hounds of God didn't seem to believe my explanations. One of them sniffed at me, growling, then backed off, showing his slavering chops. *He* knows! The divine spirit is in him, he has understood that I am neither Christian, nor believer, nor good citizen. Fortunately, the religious police are not so hard to convince. They accept my explanations. They simply impose on me, out of principle, a fine of 30 percent on the sum to be paid.

Perhaps, in the end, the money which goes into the coffers of the Neo-Christian dictatorship seems more important to them than the sincerity or simulacrum of my faith. This is not only plausible, but normal. For a long time now, no one has been able to distinguish between the spirit of Mammon and the religious metaphysic, which are the twin sources of power. One serves the other, and vice versa: that's truth.

February 5, 1999

To avoid further problems, I got up at five o'clock to present myself at the Treasury of Religious Allocations, and discuss a compromise with them to settle my debt. They granted me a delay, but I am obliged to take up with a supplementary treasury, Deferred Allocations. One cannot say it enough: the trap is well conceived; they leave no ways out, no element of chance. To put money aside is a myth of the past. No individual is allowed, any longer, to have a bank account; and, on the other hand, our purchases are strictly supervised and limited, so that we are inured to the idea that the money which the State gives us returns, in one form or another, to the State. There's only one question that we might still ask: Why do they give it to us? Probably to create a number of offices that require personnel, parasitical workers that otherwise would be in danger of unemployment, which the law expressly forbids.

February 6, 1999

It is pouring.

Whenever it rains I ask myself if it is indeed the gray sky that makes the city's ugliness stand out; whenever it's fair I believe, on the contrary, that it is the light of the beaming sun that lends this city its full range of deformity. It depends, of course. But actually, whether the sun's shining or not, the city remains equally ugly.

Everywhere in the city, the square and the straight line are the rule. The utilization of the curve and the sphere has been permanently banned, in an unappealed decision by the Center of Exact Measurements, which keeps a close watch that nothing be left to chance or inventive gratuitousness. Most of the residential cubes have six stories, but there are many double cubes, the exclusive properties of certain important offices such as the Center for Distribution of Time, the Central Identity File, the Office of Orders and Prohibitions, the innumerable collection bureaus and the many ministries that need the wings to tuck away their implacable cocoon of laws. Each commercial enterprise, like each residential building, has its own supervisory offices as well, its own files, its autonomous surveillance police, its network of special espionage; and by law, these different services occupy the ground floor, preventing access by a barrier of little windows and entrances.

The whole constitutes a spider's web, of which the true nervous center is strictly anonymous, unknown, inaccessible, buried who knows where. And even if its motor brain was cut for ever, each individual cell in the system, even the most insignificant, possesses its autonomous life, its immutable laws, and would be perfectly able to survive independently, isolated perhaps, but organized once and for all, unbreakable.

The facades of all the administrative buildings are tarred; those of residential buildings are in dark concrete, and this funereal backdrop is evidently not calculated to enliven a scene already unattractive. This measure was the direct consequence of the cleaning and scraping of all facades, a major operation which employed thousands of workers in the 1980's. Completely in vain. A year later, attacked by carbonic gases, smoke, dust, the dirt and germs of the city, the toxic products, the city once more lay under a gray shroud. It was then that a decree from the Central Bureau of Urbanism went out that everything should be made dark. One's grown accustomed to it. And it is actually less dirty. More lugubrious, but less dirty. At any rate, this decor has less presence than one might have thought, as it is permanently submerged under a sheet of dirty fog, of polluted dust, and smoke that escapes in a continuous jet from the enormous crematory blocks, where each building dumps its rubbish, its dead, its debris, and its surplus.

The interiors would be more reassuring if one were allowed to furnish them to one's taste, an initiative which has not existed for fifteen years. There are no more empty lodgings, only municipal ones furnished and supervised by the Office of Orders and Prohibitions, which controls every variation, and lets nothing escape it. The interiors all resemble each other, down to the furniture. Each piece of furniture is also riveted to the floor, and always in the same position, in rooms always arranged in the same manner. To be at home is to be in anyone's place in the city, is to be at home everywhere. Everyone is in the same boat —the same general mediocrity of depressive sobriety, of naked, cold walls, and objects reduced to prototypes of which each detail is in conformity to proven standards of functional ugliness. The sole personalization of objects is the number they bear: that of the register which is adjudged to us in place of our names, forgotten, effaced, rejected. I am 4569 18101492, which signifies that I was born on 4/5/69, that I am domiciled in compartment 18, in building 101, on 492nd Street.

Sometimes I tell myself that there must be places where life might be more agreeable, or at least better aired. But it's impossible to get the Commissariat of Travel to give you permission to change cities without a valid pretext. Impossible for an underling. When I think that I am unable even to change neighborhoods without making endless applications. And then, it's easy to say that life is more agreeable elsewhere. But death?

February 8, 1999

There were still some white or clear gray automobiles for sale. There won't be any more from next month on. Only black or dark gray automobiles will be tolerated in the streets. The Office of Orders and Prohibitions adds no comment on this news, but it was doubtless suggested by the Ministry of Preventive Measures. The trickling filth that blackens the whole city was too clearly visible on white cars. When one thinks that we accept all this! But there's still no question of our accepting *ourselves,* or changing our color to make it seem that all is well.

February 10

I have decided henceforth not to note the year. It's too monotonous. And it seems that it will not change for another year or two. The next date, then, that I'll note will be 2000. That's rather exciting—if I get as far as that. It's frightening: to be alive means, above all, asking oneself whether one will still be alive in an hour.

February 13

There are, nonetheless, days less fertile in events than others. Such as today. I must record that I got up at about seven o'clock, to learn that, after a contraction of time, it was actually seven in the evening.

I scarcely had time to brush my teeth.

February 14

This morning, the *Quotidian* appeared completely smeared with black. One mass of darkness for eight pages. A sign of mourning, no doubt. As for knowing who is dead . . . even the radio does not inform us of *that*. It observes a day of silence, equally in sign of mourning. And no foreign paper will give us a clue to the enigma. They have been banned for a long time back. No one has ever even seen the local paper of a neighboring province. One sometimes asks oneself if the rest of the world still exists.

February 17

After an evening traffic jam, one of the tunnels leading from the city was completely clogged throughout the night; and this morning they recovered two thousand asphyxiated bodies and a few dying. The final touch was that the survivors were crawling along to commandeer new cars to replace their own, irretrievable and bound for the scrap heap. The ad men digested this odd fact, and came up with a new slogan: "Think of the future and its imponderables; always have in reserve two or three rescue vehicles. Drive, and don't let yourself be driven by events." The slogan must have worked, because the lines in front of the great automobile firms throughout the city brought on bottlenecks even more spectacular than usual. We've gotten to the point where pedestrians are seriously impeding circulation.

February 19

My job as a totaler in a publishing house is getting more and more monotonous. Counting consonants, vowels, commas, and spaces for eight hours a day is rather trying. But I will have to stick to it. I've had this job for eight years, and my first raise does not come until after ten years. That's the law, and one has to comply with it. Anyway, to change jobs, I would have to send in a request to the Office of Professional Employment, and I don't think they would ever consider my case. It's too boring—they wouldn't even answer.

To distract myself at the office, I sometimes pay compliments to the young woman who, for some weeks, has been working in the same room as myself. She is mild, sad, sleepy and slightly soft. I would very much like to sleep with her, but how? I have already been unfaithful to my legitimate mistress twice in the past year, and with the assessments directly proportional, I would have to pay Sexual Allocations more than two thousand francs this time for my temporary adultery card. And nowadays, it's impossible to get through the net without this card. Impossible to go to her place or mine: all private dwellings are closely watched by the household supervisors. It has been illegal to go to a hotel with a girl since October 7, 1985, the date of the suppression of the Sexual Revolution. Of course, there might be the solution of making love on the sly in a closet at the office, if all the rooms weren't spied on by directorial television. And besides, the young woman doesn't want to do it in a closet. She finds it vulgar. And there is not even the "out" of getting drunk and forgetting this frustration at the office. Alcohol can only get you into prison, or even to the steps of the scaffold.

February 22

Good day. I found a burnt match that was lacking in my collection of disposable used things. I had long since lost hope that I would find a match of this color, and it astonishes me that I should have found it by chance, in a groove in my floor, whereas most of the rare pieces in this collection required considerable ramblings, and years of patient searching.

As a matter of fact, I'm not a particularly avid collector, but I do like to save whatever comes to hand and, without being thrifty, I've formed the habit of throwing nothing away. Thus, within the confines of the two rooms of my apartment, I have a little of everything, arranged in glass cases, or simply set on shelves: little scraps of European wood, samples of cigarette ashes, razor blades from their origins down to modern days, all-purpose nails, cocoons of various kinds of dust, household rubbish, enough stones and stuff to turn my two rooms into a rock garden, used pipes, tin cans gutted and emptied of their contents, all sorts of things, without even mentioning the rest.

An eclecticism which allows me to profit to the utmost from certain objects that most people throw away without a thought. Thus, an old packing case supplies several of my collections, since I keep the nails, the wood, the old labels, the indefinable odds and ends and, of course, the dust that one always finds in the corners, rolled into cocoons of an inexhaustible variety.

February 23

In the garrets of our building, there is no one who is receiving oxygenated air. This oversight has claimed one more victim tonight: a child whose gas mask unfortunately slipped off while he was asleep.

February 25

I don't really understand what has happened. It seems to me that my alarm clock, which I had set for the 24th, went off only on the 25th, a day late in other words. What could have happened on the 24th? I, who am never interested by anything, suddenly attach a singular importance to this day that I missed. What if it just happened to contain the one significant event of my existence? Or perhaps my death? But as for the latter event, I am very likely to encounter it another day. Besides, am I quite certain that the 24th occurred? Not very, no. I go to the Office of General Information: they suggest that I inquire at the Observatory, where I am informed that the day in question is presently under observation. They will write to me.

February 26

I stuck to my point, and requested that I live the 26th twice by way of compensation; but the Syndicate for Apportionment of Time refused me authorization. They also reminded me that I owe them four days, eight hours, twenty minutes, and twelve seconds. What could I have done to get such a high time-bill? Yet I continually have the feeling of wasting my time, never of gaining it.

February 29

In principle, the month of February should have only twenty-eight days; but it is already several years now that the Syndicate for Apportionment of Time has imposed on us a February 29th, the entire profits from which are all poured into the National Treasury. They do not tell us why, but in certain circles it's said that it is a sort of dues, contributed by all the inhabitants to pay for the damages caused by a certain revolution which took place in May 1968. Rather minor damages, anyway, from what they say: a few smashed storefronts, three trees cut down and several sidewalks damaged. It's really a bit disgusting: we are paying thirty years later for the breakages of a revolution of which no one has ever heard. The very word "revolution" seems disquieting to us, harmful, to be avoided at all costs. The last gesture of revolt that one can remember, in September 1997, took place in an office, and cost us dear: a thousand employees were shot without trial, on the spot. It's even better not to think of it. That could be dangerous. Who knows if the authorities don't have at their disposal a television that could capture the most intimate thoughts . . .

March 1

It's not only the first of March, it's Saturday again.

And so the day of my legitimate mistress' visit. I study her, and I don't recognize her. I learn that the usual woman is on a trip, and that the Office of Household Supervision has allocated a replacement to me, a close relative, it seems. As they seem to be more or less the same weight, she will bring only slight changes into my life, unless I have to pay increased support costs: this one wears a bit of makeup, and a longer skirt.

I am surprised that the adoptive cousin has also been replaced, by an unattractive-looking little girl. I preferred the other child, all in all: I'd gotten used to him.

"What happened to him?" I ask the substitute.

"He didn't work out. He's been put on Relief."

If only I could not work out, and she could turn me over also to the care of this organization. But fathers are never taken in, not even underage ones.

Like the woman whom she has replaced, she looks at me without a trace of feeling, without the slightest expression. She doesn't appear to be hungry or thirsty, and discharges her duty as you or I would go to the office. Useless to delude oneself: she will never have anything to say to me, she will never have any thoughts about me, she will never feel anything for me. And this will be mutual, obviously.

"Do you smoke?" I ask her, as if I had just met her in a train.

She shakes her head, and takes out a pencil and pad.

"Do you make love before or after eating?" she questions me, with perfect indifference.

"I prefer it before," I say, to get rid of her as soon as possible.

She makes a note of it.

"Upright? Lying down? On the stomach? From behind? In the bathroom? Under a ladder?" she continues her investigation.

"That depends. We'll have to see."

She writes nothing, and looks me up and down, to let me know that she disapproves of this kind of improvisation.

"Any special perversions?" she goes on.

I observe that she is taking her notes in shorthand, a sign of admirable professional conscientiousness.

"Tomorrow is Sunday," she adds.

A further indication, of a certain imaginativeness in the art of conversation. And, so as not to be left behind, I add:

"Ah yes. Another week over with."

Another one, good. But after? After?

March 2

It is indeed Sunday, as we foresaw.

Having found an apple seed which I did not yet possess in my collection of pits and cores, I took the occasion to do some classifying. I removed the used razor blades from their case, to put them where the cigarette ashes had been. These I placed in the case of the all-purpose nails, after having transferred *them* to the shelf of rubbish, which I took down to place in the case with the dust cocoons.

Towards evening, I took a look at the whole collection, and I have to admit that nothing has changed. Here is a Sunday well spent: it was good for nothing, and yet it passed.

March 4

It must have been 3 P.M. or so, and I'd reached page 254 of a manuscript, and a total of 312,588 punctuation marks, when darkness abruptly fell. My first idea was that the sun had broken down; but the radio soon informed us that the day had been shortened, docked of nine hours. As a repressive measure. There are more and more in these latter days, and for reasons more and more obscure. One doesn't even know who is taking them. What office, what syndicate, what bureau. . . . It is true that they are extremely many. But they all have the same purpose. And all the same complete authority. They are all at the service of an anonymous government, of which we know nothing. When one thinks that we do not even know the name of our Dictator-President. Which does not exclude the veneration that we're supposed to hold him in.

March 7

The problem of clutter in my apartment worsens from day to day. Of course, there would be space enough in the main room if, right in the middle of the other room, passing through the floor and the ceiling, there were not the two thick cement pillars that support one of the neighborhood's suspended bridges. This would be nothing if the Bureau of Public Projects didn't plan, in the very near future, to install an elevator in my apartment, to connect 492nd Street with the fourth kilometer of Bridge 15. This elevator will mean not only loss of space: seeing batches of strangers shoot through my apartment every three minutes will not be terribly agreeable. Let's hope the Comestible Provisions Service doesn't get the idea of setting up a buffet in my studio.

March 10

Okay, so the Maritime League has insisted on building lighthouses throughout the city, although it stands at least six hundred kilometers from the nearest sea. But what need was there to have these midearth lighthouses sounding their foghorns all night, exactly as if they were well out at sea? Already, the one that was put up about a thousand yards from my residence has been sweeping my apartment every ten seconds with its pale spotlight; now, in the same rhythm, it bellows the plaint of a monstrous seal that has been mortally wounded, and that will remain forever suspended between two death rattles. In the end, this will tell on the nerves as surely as the dentist's drill. But doubtless, that's what they want. To push us to the limit. The limit of what? Does anyone know? From this to having trains run through our apartments on their way nowhere is but a step.

March 11

It is today (as it is every two months) the day of the Work Break.

A gang of time-workers who work in the basement emerge from my cousin's wardrobe; for it is indeed by this entrance that the time-laborers reach their place of work, and it is also their exit when they come back up. As for knowing exactly what it is they're working on. . . . Certain people claim that they have been trying, for two years now, to repair a foul-up in time. Or one might suppose that they are simply trying to stop a time leak. Anyway, it's not very important, and to offer them a cup of coffee every two months doesn't bother me much. Their faces pale, their clothes dusty, their hands covered with the dust of time, they always seem happy to return to the surface to talk to me, not about the time they are making down below, but about the weather up above.

As for the relief workers, they enter the wardrobe in their turn, and disappear within, closing the door behind them, not without a friendly sign to me in passing.

It only remains for me to collect the residues of dust which they have left behind them on the floor. Consider all the dust of the centuries which I gather with emotion, trying in vain to distinguish between the dust of the nineteenth and eleventh centuries. I simply put it all in a vial which I lock inside the case reserved for my collection of temporal materials, already rich with a draught of bottled evening air, a conjugation in the past indefinite that somehow happened to solidify, a two-hour span of time, a scrap of the thread of life, unfortunately in poor condition, a brief interval whose exact origins I do not know and, above all, a piece of dead time that I had much trouble in retrieving.

For a moment I consider all these treasures, then my other collections: first one group, then another, then all my belongings together; and I say to myself that it's not so bad. If only all this were able to console me. If only all this were not as useless as my walls, as the sky, as love, as the invention of the rubber band or the bottomless drawer; as useless as combining form with function; as useless as anything at all. Death has definitely spoiled my entire life. Nothing of what I have experienced can console me for the certainty of dying one day. One question only remains unanswered: Will death console me for my life?

March 14

Among the expected bills, unforeseen and foreseeable, I received by this morning's post a threat of distraint from Directed Contributions. I am surprised, more frightened than surprised. They demand payment for all of 1997, whereas I have just finished making the last settlements in connection with that year. Without losing a moment, or even a second, I betake myself to the Central Treasury of Directed Contributions, and insist on my rights. It is a pleasant moment. It's not every day that one catches Contributions red-handed in an error. But I very soon have to lower my tone. An employee, who offers me an admirable view of her little municipal backside—it sends the blood rushing to my head—examines her books, briefly, for my accounts. She wheels around to inform me that I have in fact paid for 1997, but not the indexed parallels which are inversely proportional to the progressively diminishing ones of the same year. The parallels? Who could have imagined it? What exactly is it a question of? Contributions which we would be paying if we were living in two worlds at once, the other parallel to ours? Taxes which we shoulder for our double, our reflection or our ghost? Possible. In the cloudy domain of contributions, all is possible. And it's useless to ask for explanations: they will surely demonstrate to me, as in certain nightmares, by an absurd logic, that it's all perfectly normal, plausible. Once more I accept, I approve. I promise that I will pay. The employee in attendance records my agreement, takes some notes, and does not even offer me her ass in exchange for my good resolutions. All the same, how can she work for Contributions with a butt like that? To find out, I ask her if she would like to have dinner with me tonight. She doesn't answer, but a solemn male voice intones through the loudspeaker, hard by the cash register: "Your proposition will cost you a fine of three thousand francs, and one more word will mean the third degree. That clear?"

It is completely clear, and I leave without waiting to hear more.

March 22

I'm back from my week of revolutionary service, which I was called up for last Monday.

Revolutionary service has replaced military service, since the State has not participated in foreign politics for nearly fifteen years, and has refused, henceforward, to involve itself in any global conflict. But this does not prevent civil wars, which can be equally murderous, and generally more dangerous for a mother country that respects its government above all. The famous revolution of 1988 gave the authorities much to think about. In fact, it cost

more than three million dead and, most important, it
nearly overthrew the Christian Right power, so long established. It is, in fact, to prevent a similar flare-up, and
to systematically defuse amateur combatants, that each
citizen is obliged to put in a week of revolutionary service
every six months. Each time, like everyone else, I return
from them nauseated, disgusted by days of harassment
which monotonously unfold. Days filled with aggressive
slogans which one must shout at the top of one's lungs;
insults to the police; cobblestones, which one endlessly
hurls; tear-gas bombs that one takes in the mouth; moves
to vote that go on until dawn, and organizational shake-
ups that go on until evening; counter demonstrations; and
exhausting processions under banners almost too heavy to
carry. When one comes out of that, one prefers prison, in
the end, to all forms of revolution. And at the mere
thought of a procession, one has but one desire: to pro-
ceed away from it. It's not for nothing that the last protest
of 1998 against the deadly pollution of the air drew only
six people.

March 25

This morning I received a visit from an inspector from
Enforced Leisure. He didn't have a very obliging air;
everything in his attitude clearly betokened that he was
armed, not only with the full powers of his rank, but also
with a gun. After having demanded my papers, he asked
for my sports book.

"Your Tennis Club has notified us that it's more than a
month since you've been seen on the court," he said.
"You're of course aware that you are required to present
yourself at your Club more than once a week."

I do know it, I stammer. I improvise several excuses. A

slight feeling of fatigue, not much energy, worries about
my health, bad performances recently. He pays no attention and brutally interrupts me.

"No excuses will stand up. Sports are mandatory, and
you have been officially inscribed in a tennis club because
you claimed to like it. Consequently, we will impose a
severe punishment."

And so he does. I have to go play tennis every night
from nine to eleven for fifteen days. Then to resume at the
stipulated pace. This is all the more stupid in that the
more I train, the worse I play. Before, a few years ago,
only my service left something to be desired. Now, my
backhand is all fouled up, I miss every ball to my right,
I lose every volley, and my serve has never been weaker.
And tennis bores me more than the office. At least at the
office, if you have a good excuse, they simply have you
make up the lost time between noon and one, not in the
middle of the night.

March 30

As at the end of every month, I had to submit my
monthly employee's report to my President Director General. My marks are not very good, this month. Application:
nine out of twenty. Enthusiasm: three. Efficiency: six.
Conduct: at times leaves something to be desired. Particular remarks: has already done better, and ought to be
able to do better. The Director General looks me between
the eyes, to tell me that it's already more than six years
that they have been kind enough to hope that I would do
better one day.

"I note also," he informs me, "that in the course of the
month you committed a rather regrettable error. In a text
which had only 783,644 punctuation marks, you counted

783,646. This is a discrepancy of two marks. You will copy this number 100,000 times for me by tomorrow morning."

I would like to have just one day in the month without punishment. But this has never yet happened to me.

March 31

It must have been about three A.M. when two men from the Censorship Brigade broke into my apartment, revolvers in hand. Their first act was to secure me to a radiator with a pair of handcuffs.

"Where is it?" one of the policemen shouted, shoving his fist in my face.

Where is what? I was able to swear to them that I had never hidden anything or anyone in this apartment.

"Okay, okay—you don't have to play little games with us. We have information. You are known to be hiding a foreign magazine in here, a publication from America. You'd be better off confessing."

But confess what, when I don't know anything? All I know is that since the law of February 14, 1989, no one is allowed, any longer, to export, sell, buy, borrow, or read any foreign newspaper or book whatsoever. I know also that any infraction of this law means twenty years in prison. What's more, I don't read English. And I don't even know if the United States still exists: New York, it's said, was obliterated five years ago by a super H-bomb which was theoretically headed towards the Antilles. Not knowing a thing, I tell them all this.

"All right. It won't take us long to find it ourselves."

And, sure enough, in a few minutes they come up with a crumpled page from a magazine which they've culled from the dustbin. I blanch: it does, in fact, seem to be written in a foreign language. I recognize this page; it served as a wrapper for a carton of cigarettes which I bought about ten days ago. I tell them this also.

"Good. Here's your summons. You will present yourself at Screening in eight days. And watch your wrappers."

I agree, with conviction.

That is the whole secret: to say yes, to comply. To Contributions, at the office, before the police, outside, at home, day and night, one must always agree. Agree in an even voice, deferent, very steady. That way one does avoid certain problems.

April 1

Payday. I specify that the "pay" part of payday only lasted for a few seconds, after which it was taken away for remission to the coffers. It's a little farce the office plays with us to mark April Fools' Day. It must be said that this way of taking things in the spirit of the letter is rather amusing, and we all laughed a lot. It reassures me to see that this office, which is said to be severe and gloomy, still cultivates a certain sense of humor on certain occasions.

Having said this, I ask myself how I am going to live this month.

April 3

In the depths of a cupboard, I have four 33 rpm records which my father willed to me, and which I have never been able to listen to. It seems that these records were played, during the 70's, on machines that ran on electricity. The State banned these machines twenty years ago, judging them to be subversive. It seems, in fact, that on these machines—which were called phonographs—one could listen to whatever one wanted to hear, even the most violent texts. One simply had to place a record beneath the needle, and set it running along the grooves, in order to hear what had been inscribed, once and for all, in the wax surface. And one could listen to what had been recorded any number of times, endlessly, to the end of time. This seems scarcely believable in a period when the national radio alone is the law. This single, uniform program that one can listen to only once. Luckily. Once is enough for everyone, and how! One can only believe that records were more interesting. But how can one know for sure when no one will ever be able to hear them again. The labels remain on these records. I read: Louis Armstrong, Lester Young, Charlie Parker, Duke Ellington. But what do these names represent? Singers, orators, politicians, assassinated presidents, actors, monologuists? One will never know, since their records are mute, without purpose, dead, abstract, unusable. This is perhaps to be regretted. Or is it perhaps not better to wonder, as one thinks about these names, whose syllables vaguely evoke a foreign language forever prohibited to us? It seems that my father possessed more than two thousand records, and all different from each other. What a pity that he didn't will me the machine on which one could listen to them. Useless to ransack the city to find one. For a long time the phonograph has figured in the blacklist of forbidden objects. It would even be better not to rummage in stray cupboards to unearth, by miracle, one of these relics of the past. To use it would mean immediate arrest by the Bureau of Orders and Prohibitions. And how one can always count on a neighbor, an acquaintance, or a relative to denounce you in the nick of time! . . . How could it be otherwise with those monthly bonuses for stool pigeons, which General Supervision takes pleasure in distributing.

April 5

It is nonetheless curious to think that, for more than twenty years now, we have lived, not merely in a closed society, completely sealed off within the prison of our frontiers, thrown back on an eternal present, but that the government has cut off all contact with the past, and destroyed all proof that this past ever existed. For the old scholar as for the young student, the history of the world begins in 1980, the year one of the Christian Right Regime. Of former times, the "before" of prehistory up to 1980, there is nothing. Nothing but a deluge of bad examples to be expunged from our memories, to be forgotten entirely under penalty of deportation. If one must choose, it's better to deport one's memory. And to accept what they say, what they offer you, what they sell, without looking further. It isn't happiness, but neither is it the misery that strikes faster than lightning here. Besides, when one rejects one's imagination, one easily accepts anything. Thus, who can prove to us that there *was* something before 1980? That the world already existed, that the flow of history was a single wave of violence and madness, wars and outcries, storms and spasms. No one can prove it to us. No one could ever furnish us with the proof of it, not even by ransacking the most secret archives of the city. Well, then?

April 10

It's a day off, without being a holiday. But the State Radio today is broadcasting the quarterly speech of our President-Dictator, which we must listen to. I even ask myself to what extent the dead can escape it. Someone could rig up a loudspeaker underground in their coffins, without it surprising me overly. One sole favor in connection with this speech: We are allowed to listen to it at home, but without occupying ourselves with any diversion or leisure task. We must sit facing the loudspeaker on the wall, listening, or at least pretending to listen. And since, on this day in particular, there are a great many helicopters of Political Surveillance skimming the windows to see that there are no infractions, it's in everyone's best interest to observe the letter of the law. The speech lasted six hours, as usual. It resembled, in every point, that of the last quarter, which exactly recalled that of the preceding quarter, and so on. In a general, vague, and extremely roundabout way, the President affirmed that all was going well, that all would go better and better in the very near future; that the rises would pursue their normal course, that the active would balance the passive, and that the country had never known such austerity in prosperity, nor a greater prosperity in austerity.

I suppose that the fifteen million inhabitants were very happy to learn that they were all very happy. Sometimes it's these little encouragements that help you to live.

April 12

Today, at the office, we celebrated the transfer of our Chief Accountant who has been named Assistant Accountant at Higher Supervision of Frauds. A promotion the honor of which is reflected on all the personnel. As for myself, I believe that I will remain a totaler all my life, and in the same company, since no one is allowed to change employment of his own will. It is the Office of Distribution of Labor that decides, and it does not have the reputation of making its decisions lightly. My meager capacities as a subaltern fourth class prohibit me, at any rate, from making an official request for an eventual change. It would be necessary for me to advance to at least the second class, which I have been trying vainly to do for many years.

The celebration ended with a speech, which summarized, in several hours, the rather monotonous life of our colleague; after which, we were entitled to a dessert which did not appear on the office menu. A little surprise, as it were.

This also often seems rather monotonous to me: this obligation to eat your two daily meals on the company premises, meals invariably composed of soup, a piece of meat with raw apples, and a chunk of cheese. When one thinks that there used to be many restaurants in the great cities, and that one could choose the dishes one wanted! But the noonday meal, frugal though it is, does afford a brief hour of respite, and that of the evening, a half hour. After the coffee sprinkled with powdered tranquilizer, there is the technical conference which lasts from 8 to 10 p.m. and deals with the most diverse subjects, ranging from management to the environment, from bookkeeping to profit making, from parking to marketing. We are all required to attend these. On the other hand, the complementary meeting, which lasts until midnight, is optional. Most of the employees attend it regardless, either to avoid the early-hour traffic jams, or because they don't really know what to do at home.

April 13

Personally speaking, one of my few pleasures would be reading. I am not able to satisfy this vice in the publishing house that employs me. It does publish a single pamphlet, the *Official Journal*, the sole survivor of the press of the past. It should be said that even when one wants to read, one feels some weariness in being swamped by an eternal deluge of decrees, decisions, resolutions, and motions.

What is there, then? Absolutely nothing, aside from the Book of the Week, for which everyone is officially subscribed. Rather austere reading, almost always. Most of the time, I have great trouble finishing the Book of the Week, whose subjects are always functional, and very arid. I take a few works at random: *Faith in Faith, The Son, the Exchequer, and the Fiscal Policy, The Environment at the Office, Efficiency and Non-Efficiency, The Circulation of the Blood in Circulation, The Function of the Functional*. Truly, none of these works is very appealing. One rarely feels like re-reading them.

April 18

An employee of our company was arrested this morning by the Excess Brigade. It's whispered that he will not get less than ten years in prison. That is, if he doesn't get twenty years in Parallel Labors, which is scarcely more desirable. Reason: out of bravado or an impulse to revolt, he came in wearing an orange sweater, when aside from black and gray all colors are strictly prohibited. All the same, one asks oneself where he found the dye—in what forgotten depths of a bureau drawer. To wear something colored: what an idea! When one thinks that, for so long already, the city had been having all trees felled, and all lawns demolished whose greenness made us think of vacations, weekends, laziness, and time to lose in loafing. Colors have vanished from store windows, from advertising posters, from shopfronts, and interiors. In a general way, in our universe of black stones, gray sidewalks, and gray skies, only two patches of color are still tolerated: red lights and green lights. These are bright touches, it must be admitted.

April 20

As often happens, the Center for Distribution of Time canceled a day, the 19th of April. But it was a Sunday, just the one day that entitles us to an afternoon of rest. Strange, but when the Center cancels one of our days, it's almost always a Sunday. I sometimes ask myself if this isn't deliberate.

April 21

There will be no more Sundays for a month. After a case of cheating on a paid day off, the Syndicate for Apportionment of Time has decided to punish us severely, and thus regain the lost time. Thus, the entire week is working days for everyone until May 21st.

April 25

Next Sunday, that is to say in a month, I will be able to go to the movies. I have just received my admission ticket, which we are entitled to once every quarter. There are only three theaters in the whole city; that's not many for fifteen million inhabitants, but it's better than nothing, and cinema does not interest everyone. It should be said that it is not very interesting, not much more than the literature; but what will one not accept by way of distraction? I've chosen the program at the Gray Palace: *A Working Day*, which relates, with a realism which is said to be gripping, the day of an employee in accounts, charged with addressing envelopes. Luckily, the film only lasts four hours, not ten. All in all, I would be better off, perhaps, in going to see *Post Office and Police,* which depicts the ruthless inquiry conducted by the inspectors of the postal brigade to discover the unscrupulous employee who stole a dozen stamps. One should, nonetheless, mistrust those films one believes will be exciting. Last February, I went to see *Identity Card,* attracted by the title, but the film merely showed the three hour wait of a man who had lost his papers, and was requesting others.

As for television, it is a good two years since I have looked at any program. Anyway, there *is* only *one* program, twenty-four hours a day, and always the same: various shots taken in the street, of a single, permanent traffic jam, and one continuous procession of cars. All this without commentary, of course: this is beyond it. It seems that this interminable sequence impassions motorists, who gorge themselves on it from the moment they leave their cars. As for myself, since I do not have a car, it bores me. Fortunately, I do not live too far from my place of work; by subway, it does not take more than two hours.

May 2

False move on the part of the Center for Distribution of Time? Temporal depression? A hole in time? One will never know; all the more because no one ever dreams of giving us the slightest explanation. But the whole city lost its memory during the week that has just passed. What could have happened since April 26th? Did something happen? No one will ever know. A week like a black hole, into which fifteen million inhabitants have fallen. Perhaps we were thrown back into a distant past during those few days? Or perhaps, on the contrary, we made a leap into the future, the very depths of a future which we will never live; and all this to suddenly return to our gloomy present? And even if we did nothing but live in our present, things remain nonetheless heavy with questions. Some have committed offenses of which they have no memory, and for which they will pay one day. Others have met the woman of their life, but they will never find her again. Couples dazedly ask themselves what they are doing together in bed, while young women ask themselves why they are alone in theirs. Millions of employees stumble through their daily work, deprived of the coordinates of the day before, cut off from everything. Innumerable motorists ask themselves in vain where they could have left their cars. Manufacturers conduct inquiries as to whether they have made their payments.

For me only, this week of total darkness is without mystery. Since nothing ever happens in my life, there isn't much reason for anything to have happened precisely between April 26th and May 2nd. I am not dead, that at least seems certain. I don't feel better than last week, nor less well. I still have the same head and the same necktie. Same shirt, too. Deprived of memory, I forgot to change them. In short, everything is as it was. I feel no dislocation, and I am tormented by no deep questions. The general loss of memory will leave me as many memories as my memory in the end.

May 5

The nocturnal visits of the investigators are growing more and more frequent. And for some time now, they have been waking people up between three and five in the morning. This must be the tenth time that they have taken the exact measurements of every room in my apartment, which can puzzle you if you know that all the apartments in the city have the same measurements, the same standard disposition of furniture. What exactly do these investigations means? And who orders them? The Bureau of Orders and Prohibitions? The Office of Preventive Investigation? A department which nobody knows about? To conduct an investigation of this subject might be useful. But dangerous. Therefore to be avoided.

To my mind, these surveyors are taking notes other than the ones they pretend to be taking. They come to smell out the inside of the apartments. To see if one doesn't possess some forbidden, old, or unusual object. To check whether anything is fastened to or hung on the walls, which must remain white, empty, immaculate, as virgin as the void. To be sure that no one owns any other works than the complete collection of the Books of the Week. In the final analysis, they're assuredly sent by the Center for General Supervision of Particulars. Of which I'll say nothing. If there is one Center that does not fool around, it's this one.

May 10

One of the anonymous journalists of the *Quotidian* was evidently condemned to death last month. Neither the paper nor the radio announced the news, but public rumor spread it. According to what they say, this journalist, in a moment of aberration, wrote an article directly attacking the gas pollution of the cities, and advocating a return to electrically powered cars—silent, economic, and harmless for the population which nowadays one might call the "pollulation." Not only was his article never published, but the Ministry of Profits, which derives directly from the

National Gas Office, demanded the arrest and then the immediate condemnation of the journalist. His name will drop forever into oblivion, since it is a long time now that martyrs have been denied the right to statues or portraits. Nonmartyrs also, it must be said. In a world of registers and tickets, of tariffs and account books, men, whether they are leading or led, no longer have names. They may no longer serve to designate streets, squares, cities, dishes, or objects. Numbers have replaced them. Numbers, which are mute, speak for them. They speak, but say nothing.

May 14

The Regulating Committee on Climates has announced its intention, starting next year, to move warm air into the city in winter, and cold air in summer. But I don't see very well what this can signify. When we have heat waves in December, and night frost in July, we won't be much further along. It is true that if we gain nothing from the exchange, we don't lose anything either. One might say that this is almost a compensation.

May 15

I was summoned by the chief inspector of the company which employs me. It had been some time since this had happened to me, and I was rather uneasy.

"Well?" the inspector said to me. "You forget everything?"

I had to say that I so often forget things that I'd completely forgotten what I might have forgotten in particular on this day.

It was less serious than I could have imagined. I had

simply omitted to buy the ticket for the Worker's Lottery which every job holder is obliged to buy each week.

"I'm extremely sorry I forgot," I said to excuse myself.

This cost me a week's stoppage of pay, whereas I might have won a week's salary if my ticket had been drawn. But I have never seen a winning ticket drawn. It's said that the chances of a winning ticket being drawn are one in ten million. But what does it matter, in the end, when one thinks of how unexciting the stakes are.

May 16

Yesterday I may have lost a week's salary, but I have recovered a day's salary by way of a bonus offered by the Radio, in connection with their Wednesday radio games. It is in fact the first time that I have answered the first, correctly, to one of the questions that we are deluged with throughout Wednesday. It must be said that the question was easy for me. Almost as if it had been made to order. They asked how many punctuations marks the last issue of the *Official Journal* contained. Child's play, really: I had just set the type for it the day before last. It reassures me a little, since in general the barrage of questions concerning municipal laws or working techniques, salaries and taxation, accounting procedures, or the labor culture leave me without an answer, and quite perplexed. I am happy, above all, to have been able to prove my assiduity in listening, since to be suspected of never taking part in the weekly games can entail heavy surtaxes, which Complementary Contributions takes pleasure in adding to Directed Contributions.

May 19

Saturdays at the office, we are, extraordinarily, allowed to leave at seven o'clock, to give us time in which to make our weekly purchases.

Today, this works out well, since I am looking for a new lampshade and an ashtray, strictly commonplace objects which I am obliged to buy only in my neighborhood, the one section in which my buyer's card is valid. Since little shops all vanished after the great commercial reform of 1993, there remain at our disposition only great stores where one finds everything, whether it's a bunch of leeks or an electric bulb, a pair of shoes or razor blades. It all depends on how much one wants to pay. This means choosing between three kinds of stores: the *One Low Price* which sells at low prices, the *Middle Price,* and the *Monoluxe*. The designs in the three stores resemble each other, equally hideous, with a few variations merely in their trimmings. Personally, I nearly always opt for the *Middle Price*, which offers objects of a slightly better make than those of *One Low Price,* and less heavily taxed than those of *Monoluxe*. As far as ashtrays go, the choice is simple. In the three stores, one model is sold, made of transparent plastic, oval rather than square, and guaranteed fireproof. The choice of the lampshade doesn't pose much more of a problem. There are only two models on the market: the parchment style shade for standing lamps, and the parchment style for wall lamps. Which of the two is the most ugly? Or the least ugly? Questions truly without importance in a world where functional ugliness alone is the rule, the decor, and even the decoration. But every cloud has a silver lining: this way, one wastes little time in making purchases; one selects in a few seconds the object which one needs, one knows the price by heart, one pays, and takes it without elation or discontent. And there's no question of coming to regret one's purchase: it's the only thing for sale.

May 23

It has been a very long time since this has happened to me: In the subway, coming back from work, I met a young woman who really attracts me, whom I want and could doubtless love. We got off at the same station, and exchanged a few words. We spent a few moments on the station bench, but an inspector of Underground Customs asked us to move on, remarking that the subway was not a hotel. We wanted nothing better than to go to a hotel, but the young woman owes more than five thousand francs to Sexual Allocations. These are not the conditions under which she could request a temporary adultery card. She is a secretary, and admits the same indifferent contempt for her legitimate lover as I feel for my legitimate mistress. With this difference, that they live together, under the Daily Plan, which obviously makes things more difficult to bear. We don't know what to do with our bodies, our mouths, and our hands. We don't know where to go. We can't even go for a soft drink at one of the municipal cafés, where only legitimate couples are admitted. It is 10 P.M. We decide to see each other again the day after tomorrow: Sunday. It's my day for movies, and I am allowed one guest of my choice. Before leaving her, I flatten her against the wall of a driveway, I embrace her with all my teeth, crushing her to me. I tear off some of her buttons to touch her flesh, then I tear myself away from her, before we're caught red-handed by the Sidewalk Brigade. That would be good for several months in prison.

May 25

We met each other in front of the ten-door entrance of the Gray Palace which, with its twenty thousand seats, is the largest of the town's three theatres. The Office of Entertainment had changed the program and, instead of *A Working Day*, imposed *The Choice*, which dates from 1996, but which we are forced to see over and over again, for reasons which escape me. *The Choice* relates the rather boring story of the petty terrors of a man who doesn't know what brand of car to choose, torn between two almost identical models. One way or another, it didn't matter much to me on this day. My only thought was to lick, smell, and touch the young woman with whom I was lost in this vast cocoon of overpopulated plush.

We managed to find a nook in the very back of the room, in an almost darkened corner; but even there one had to be careful. One doesn't fool with morality at cinemas, and the pale beam of the Youth Protection Spotlight can always find you and bring you back to reality.

Fortunately, the film lasts for more than three hours; nothing but automobile trials unfold for more than two and a half hours; and approaching centimeter by centimeter, never forgetting to appear to be attentively following the film, I manage, after an hour, to cleverly lift my companion's slip. My hand plunges between her thighs, engulfed, tormented, lubricated, transformed to a fish in great depths. The young woman trembles with pleasure, sits up very straight, stiffened on the edge of orgasm. If the cars weren't making such an uproar, insensately relayed by super hi-fi, one would hear nothing in the room but the short breath of the young woman whose hand, relentless as a metronome, is scratching at my stomach.

I have never felt such a desire to get a girl down on the ground and implacably split her in two equal parts. But how to do it, how to do it? Our hands fidget and writhe together, then fall apart exhausted, limp with the same pleasure. I shut my eyes, straining. What a mess! I have never experienced such a reveling acuity of sensations with my legitimate mistresses. And no divorce is allowed before five years: I have just recently had my last.

May 28

Since it is my right to have one visit at home a month, I invited a colleague from work to spend the evening at my place. Being classed in the "hetero-normal" category, I'm only entitled to a male colleague: no question of asking a female colleague.

He arrives towards nine o'clock, as the regulations provide, and he should not leave after eleven o'clock, as provided for by the same Regulations of Private Visits.

We talk a little. This is not so easy, and we know it. We are directly connected by microphone to the Concierge-Supervisor, who records all our conversations: no need to draw a reprimand which would be directly transmitted to Allusions Control, one of the severest bureaus in the city.

After listening to the Radio, which tonight is rebroadcasting an anthology of office noises—this to get us started —we attempt to exchange a few phrases.

"How hard we've worked for the past fifteen days at the office," my guest says.

The glacial voice of the concierge rises, transmitted by the apartment's loudspeaker:

"You would be better off with a subject other than work," we're informed.

"How was the film you saw the other day? Good?" my guest asks.

"I'd already seen it the year before. Yes, not bad," I say.

"No criticisms," the concierge remarks to us.

For ten minutes, we manage to talk about the weather that doubtless lies ahead, then of the weather as it might have been, and finally of the weather as it was, without drawing a single remark. Encouraged, we venture to discuss the problem of traffic.

"Forbidden subject this week," the concierge dryly cuts in.

We detour, towards the eternal subject: cuisine and food supply. We let ourselves be carried away.

"I still think the office restaurant might vary its menus from time to time," I say.

My guest agrees. He detests boiled potatoes, and has been eating them every day for ten years.

"It's the evening dessert that I can't stand. The eternal yogurt. I end up thinking I'm still at my mother's breast."

"And the mineral water, morning, noon, and night. How long is it now that wine has been banned in restaurants?"

"It must be ten years, at least."

Three minutes later, two policemen burst into the room.

"Private Conversation Brigade," one announces.

"You talk about the past, you parade your regrets, you recriminate. Are you crazy, or what? In the end you'll revolt! Follow us, both of you."

And we follow them. Ten days in prison for attempted mutiny. If I'd known that I would land in jail anyway, I would have preferred it to be for making love to a young woman in a public place. It's true that on a charge like that I would have gotten twenty years.

June 8

I've been released from prison, and can return to the office.

But I truly have the sensation of never having left the office, because in prison every morning they bring you the work which you would have had to take on at the office. Only one difference: after 8 P.M. one is not entitled to the traditional conference on work and its substitutes. A privation which did not exactly seem overwhelming to me. As for the food, give or take a gram of meat or bread, it's exactly like the food in the office canteen. Except that the penitentiary restaurant seemed less lugubrious to me. Everything considered, I ask myself whether I would not be happier in prison than elsewhere.

June 9

Only one inconvenience: the bill for incarceration that I owe the Syndicate for Apportionment of Time. The days in prison, although I was fully employed and accountable, count for nothing, and I owe them to the Syndicate exactly as if I'd been ill, in an accident, or a simple deserter. My bill for 1999 has already climbed to fourteen days, ten hours, thirty-two minutes, and four seconds. And this is only in June. What will I owe them from here to the end of the year? They'll have to give me an intercalated month so I can repay them this avalanche of time!

June 13

A very young employee who has been working in my office for several months approached me this morning and said he had something to show me. He spoke in a low voice, and I didn't care for the precautions he took. One of my friends was condemned to death three months ago, for keeping a rusty old revolver in a drawer, in memory of his father.

The employee drew me into a storeroom. He took out a black object, gleaming, on the large side, rather ugly, and very nonutilitarian looking.

"I found it in a wardrobe under a pile of old blankets. What is it? I have never seen an object like this. Do you think it's worth something?"

I smile. I understand, in fact, that he is only sixteen years old, and has never had a chance to see this perfectly ordinary object. I, who am thirty years old, I know what it is. But how to explain it to him? It would take a long time, and no doubt be dangerous.

"It's a telephone," I say.

"A tele what? What was it used for?"

I tell him quickly, without going into details. The telephone, which seemed so ordinary to me in my childhood, was in fact banned everywhere from 1982 on. Abruptly and completely, forever. To allow people to communicate with each other in an underground, invisible, and insidious manner was a permanent risk which the government could no longer take. The State lived in the fear of an eternal conspiracy. There was of course a system of bugging in force for many years. But everyone had a telephone, and the bugs could not record all the conversations. There was only one solution: simply outlaw the telephone. That is what they did. And one learned to do without it. Without this and so many other things, if one thinks about it.

A telephone! It's a very long time since I've seen one. It doesn't make me feel any younger. Nevertheless, if we still had the phone, this evening I could call the young woman I've just met, and tell her, for lack of something better, that I want her, that my hands clench thinking of her thighs, that I would like to sink deep inside her, to drown there, to be nothing but flotsam in that torrid, sticky marsh. That would be better than nothing, at least. Better than the bare wall that I face tonight. Than the radio loudspeaker which will broadcast a program of forced praises to the glory of the latest car, on sale for the past few days.

June 24

From time to time I see the young woman about whom I think so often. I tried to bring her up to my apartment by eluding the vigilance of the concierge-supervisors, but I botched it. This attempted sexual fraud cost me a fine of a thousand francs. If I had a car, or if she had one, we could at least jabber some semblance of love talk in a closed vessel. At least, we would have some time to ourselves. Between eight and midnight, one must allow more than two hours to drive up—or down—a major artery, and at least an hour to get from one end of a traffic jam to the other at an important crossing. But we do not have a car and, in any case, the patrol cars of the Morale Brigade keep a very close watch on what goes on inside the citizens' cars. And useless to think of taxis. Any improper gesture is expressly forbidden, and each taxi driver is at once a spy, informer, and sworn policeman. When I take a taxi, I give my address and say nothing more during the trip.

June 28

The Ministry of Leisure has sent me my vacation slip. I am lucky this year. I am able to take the week of my long vacation in the month of July. My departure has been set for July 3rd. Last year I got my week in the middle of November. In Brittany, in November, it is really not very warm, and there are few things to do. But what's to be done about it? One does not take one's vacation when one is ready; one takes it when the government says so. Each citizen is entitled to a week, neither more nor less according to the rules of a very strictly controlled vacation schedule. It's been this way for five years now, since the famous year when the return *en masse* at the end of August, of tens of millions of vacationers, caused such congestion on the roads that the social life of the entire country was disrupted for more than a month. The government reacted strongly, by creating the Ministry of Leisure, which took firm and decisive measures: no more than a week of vacation, scheduling throughout the year, and mandatory vacation sites, designed in advance to avoid all surprises, and all risks of congestion.

My vacation slip assigns me to a stay in Mimizan, in Landes, on the Atlantic coast. I am happy to see that they're sending me to a region I'm unfamiliar with. It only remains to go to the Central Office of Mandatory Leave after tomorrow to pay my vacation tax, which is proportional to the distance that I must cover to get from the capital to my vacation site. It will be expensive: it's far.

July 4

I arrived at Mimizan in the night.

I got up at seven in the morning to go admire the ocean, and to look over the little town that had been assigned me for vacation in 1999. But I saw nothing at all. A gigantic sheet of fog covered the sea, the sky, and the landscape.

Of course I didn't get a bit of sleep in the night. I was officially lodged in a sort of bathhouse, which is doubtless nothing more than a sounding box constructed of plastic and formica. The least twinge of the bedsprings made the whole room creak; a shoe hitting the floor seemed to cleave the parquet asunder. What's more, the lodgings stand at the intersection of two national highways, across from a garage, and alongside a shed where twenty or so television sets are stored, going full blast and rhythmically shaking.

Towards noon, the fog finally lifted, and I noted that there was no landscape for it to hide. There is nothing here aside from sky, sand, and water farther than one can see. The bathing station, two or three hundred habitable rabbit hutches and tool sheds converted to bungalows, is apparently situated in a vast wasteland. The inland part doesn't seem to exist; they must have relegated it to even farther inland. The beach is vast, but there are more tin cans, greasy wrappers, and other debris of consumption than shells. There is a scarcely perceptible breeze, but the sea is breaking on the beach in enormous rollers, foaming, and making it impossible to swim. Besides, the DANGER flag is flying at the very top of its pole. I ask myself what flag they put up when there's a storm. The thunder of the waves is deafening, and the prospective bathers are doing nothing but listen to the uproar, in a sort of thoughtful torpor. For a moment I watch a girl dip her foot into the foam; she takes one step in; the water is now up to her ankles, and before you can say it, a wave falls on her, drags her down, and rolls her away. Three lifeguards, secured by rope, dive in after her and bring her out more dead than alive. The bathers observe the scene without even getting up. It must be commonplace: one of the few distractions of the village.

In the afternoon, the wind rises, and it is too cold to remain on the beach. Most of the vacationers gather along the National Atlantic Highway to watch the waves of traffic. Their favorite game is to read the numbers on the license plates, and to count up the cars from the capital against the provincial cars. This distracts them. Others take a nap, waiting for mealtime in the great vacationers' restaurant, a repast that resembles, almost to the last noodle, what we get regularly back at the company. Still others group themselves around public television, to bathe themselves in lukewarm jets of the monotonous, rhythmic belly-rumbling that passes for music nowadays. So-called Music to Relax By, which one can only hear at bathing stations, never in the city, where it is thought that it would distract people from working.

July 5

The Center for Distribution of Time had announced that time would be variable today. This was an understatement. The whole day, July 5, was catapulted into a day already past, June 5. For twenty-four hours, we were all living on two planes, which followed each other in defiance of all logic, and shifted back and forth with disquieting rapidity. Since I had spent June 5 at the office and was spending this day by the sea, the transitions were fairly spectacular. Once, I found myself in a bathing suit in the office of my editor in chief. Another time, I found myself sitting at my work table, whose legs were lapped by sea foam. Above all, I was struck by one fact: The day of vacation seemed hardly more attractive than the day of work.

July 6

I passed the morning by letting the morning pass.

At noon, two men from the Committee of Enforced Leisure came to call on me. They seemed solicitous, yet severe.

"You have, then, nothing to distract yourself with?" they asked me.

"Well, I've only just arrived . . ."

"We've been observing you for two days, and you really seem at loose ends. You have your papers?"

I show them my papers. They note that I am a totaler in a publishing house. They are surprised.

"You've been given no vacation exercise for these eight days? Not even any penmanship or diagrammatic exercises?"

No, I really hadn't been. They begin by noting the fact in my vacation report. This will further lower my average, at the year's end.

"We will have to notify the Bureau of Work without Remunerative Goal in connection with your case."

I say nothing, but I might have reassured them that I am used to various bureaus being notified about me. I have had so much trouble for so long with the contributions and the authorities, the detection services and supervisory offices, the syndicates for recidivists and bureaus of recall, that I am astonished at remaining anonymous on this planet when thousands of employees have had occasion to see me, to talk to me, and discuss my case.

"I must notify you," one of them concluded, "that if you do not devote yourself either to work or distractions, you will have to pay the tax for absolute idleness. And you may well believe that it is rather high, here."

I believe it readily. When they talk to me about taxes, I take them at their word.

July 7

Bureaucracy does not let up in the bathing stations. I have already been summoned by the Bureau of Work without Remunerative Goal.

They inform me that work and leisure must balance each other, that their alliance alone can produce harmony, and that in no case must the week of long vacation lead to idleness. To convince me of these basic truths, I am assigned to a busywork job where I will work from 4 to 8 P.M. on a vacation timetable for subordinate employees. That's the category I belong to.

My work is simple and rather monotonous, doubtless a little too simple. I write addresses on envelopes. Imaginary addresses, always the same, to simplify everything, since these envelopes are not meant to be mailed. They are handled by another group of employees who open them, and then return them, so that the envelopes may be used a second time. After which, they're destroyed. This employs other vacationers as well, also subject to aimless labor. I suppose no one can escape it. No one thinks anything about it, no one complains. Habit has become our sole temperamental disposition. I do think they might have given me a room with a view of the sea. Then, at least, one would have a vague feeling of holiday. Whereas this panoramic view of this concrete cube across the way really does remind you too much of the city. But doubtless that is the secret aim: never to have us lose contact, never to truly leave.

July 8

No question of going out today. Too bad, because the weather is splendid for the first time in the past few days.

But every eight days the Ministry of Public Health orders a day of complete rest for all vacationers without exception. For twenty-four hours it is expressly forbidden to stick your nose out of doors. One must remain in bed, in a state of total inactivity. One is not even entitled to go to the bathing-station restaurant. This shows with what jealous care our health is guarded, and what efforts are made to return us to city life in perfect physical and mental condition.

July 9

It is also with this in mind that the local Bureau of Sexual Affairs grants us one adultery over the vacation, with a woman of our choice. One only, and mine's set for today.

"Of one's choice" is easily said; but one short day in which to make my choice is not much time. I head for the beach, and there I take in the situation. Nearly all the young women are accompanied by their legitimate lovers, and hardly seem disposed to enjoy the rights which the vacation law allows them. They have long since been deadened in their innate frigidity, asleep in the sticky tepidity of their legal liaison, resigned to everything, sterilized, castrated of all curiosity. To sprawl in the gray sand of the beach suffices them, seems to satisfy their most savage instincts. Most of these women are as gray as the sand, besides. If only the woman whom I left in the city could be here. Then I could finally make love to her, recapture in a few moments all that we will never know together. But her week of vacation comes in December, this year, and she has to spend it by the English Channel.

I stroll along the beach, staring at each woman, weighing her body with my eye. I approach a tall blonde whose slenderness has something sad in it, rather moving. I ask her the question. She politely refuses. She would be delighted to, but she has already made love the week before, and is still quite fatigued. I go further down the beach. I approach another, less blonde, with big breasts and buttocks, rather obscene in fact. She offers her regrets, even sincerely, but after an offense committed at the start of the year, she has had her permission to sleep with anyone withdrawn for two years. I leave her to her lot. Between those who are too young or too old, too fat or too skinny, too small or too big, what is there to decide on? I consult with one whose face, breasts, and bottom please me.

"Would you like to take advantage of your vacation adultery with me?" I say, very courteous.

"Why not?" she says, rather indifferently.

She explains that she has just separated from her legitimate lover, and that she is engaged to a new lover who has already taken his week by the sea in February. So much the better. She is really rather good looking, sleek as a refrigerator, and scarcely less cold.

We walk back towards my quarters. The supervisory concierge punches our two adultery cards, and lets us pass.

She undresses, and slips between the sheets. She seems almost as beautiful to me naked as in a bathing suit. I lie down on her and shove my hand under her neck.

"Mind my hair," she says.

I remove my hand, and am about to place it over one of her breasts when she declares:

"No. I hate people playing with my breasts."

My hand descends to her belly, then lower.

"You make me sick," she asserts in a tone of voice as calm as if she were giving me the time.

No longer knowing just where to put my hand, I knead her fascinating rump.

"I can't stand it when people touch my ass," she specifies.

For lack of anything better, I grab the sheet and plunge

with my full weight into the innermost recess of the young woman, who makes me welcome without batting an eyelid. I have almost the sensation of sinking into the cold folds of an inflatable mattress—nothing more nor less. The bed moves more than my companion. It at least has a mattress which creaks, springs which vibrate. I retire, discouraged.

"Thank you, miss," I say. I don't think we are meant to understand each other.

She gets up and dresses, without making the least comment.

"See you around, maybe," she says to me before leaving.

And there's no question of looking for another partner. My adultery card is already punched, and it is only good for one time. One must resign oneself to it; after all, it's nothing much.

July 10

The weather has never been so beautiful, but during the night a monstrous whale of several hundred tons was stranded on the beach at low tide, giving off a smell of decay which threatens the entire district. Nothing to do but to hole up in our rooms, behind closed doors and windows.

July 12

I have returned to the office. This week of vacation leaves me without regrets. But, with or without regrets, I have to pay the price: for an entire month to take on two hours of supplementary work which I owe the office so as to make up the lost time. If this week of vacation was not obligatory, I believe I would refuse it. *To refuse*, yet another obsolete term, without use in a world where no one asks for your opinion.

July 14

An inspector from Leisure came to the office this morning. It was me he wanted to see.

"You're looking for trouble, no doubt about that," he informed me. "It seems that you have not been seen on the tennis courts once during the past week."

"I was on vacation."

"Exactly. Don't you know that you were supposed to report to the Tennis Club at your bathing station?"

I confess to him that I didn't know that there was a Club at the station where I'd been sent.

"There is no bathing station without a Tennis Club. You have a letter of excuse, at least? A ministerial exemption?"

Nothing at all, and I tell him so.

"You are ordered to report to the courts after work from tomorrow on. Is that clear? And you will play every day for two months."

"I'll be there."

What else can one say? One really has to go, because if one doesn't, then one is sent elsewhere, and it might be worse down there.

"I'm pleased to tell you that, for this, your sporting contributions will be heavy this year. They'll make a dent in your budget," he concluded.

Yes, yes. I am just as used to making forced contributions to Contributions.

July 18

"I'm glad to see you again," murmured the young

woman whom I'd met in the subway, and whom I found again in the same subway.

I too am happy to have found her again. It must be the first time that I've felt pleasure in brushing against a human being, a desire to talk, to touch, to give and to take. This is doubtless what one could call an emotion. Something vague, troubled, and disquieting that seems arisen from the depths of a past forever whelmed, a past of which I have forgotten all.

In a world of mediocre employees, tamed herbivores, amoebae on legs with cold little hands; in a world in which there remain only two races, the resigned subordinates and responsible aggressors, she seems to me to be descended from another race, of which we have lost the history, the morphology, the truth, and the definition. To what unidentified race does this stranger belong? And how has she received authorization to come here? What impossible bureau permitted it, what secret office? And how did she succeed in crossing the strict frontier that separates the plausible and the impossible? What visa had she obtained? And if she did not receive an official visa, how is it that she has not yet been arrested, locked up, liquidated?

I look at her with more attention than ever; I say nothing, but I am thinking nonetheless. While all the passengers on this train, and all the other trains in the city, reek of the terrestrial, the earthly, the earthy, and the dirty; while all of them amply merit the description "without identifying marks" on their I.D.'s, she alone exudes, through all her pores, the unfathomable and the disdainful, darkness and light, orgasm and frigidity, silent revolt and arrogant panic. It's enough to follow the look she gives things—the cruel, sly look of a cat who has seen a sparrow pass within reach of its claws. It's enough to enter this look, in which so many nocturnal colors are diluted that one would believe oneself mired in a nightmarish swamp. It's enough to breathe in the odor of shock at her neck, to sense the moist warmth given off by her calm female body, to lose oneself in the shadows of her great waters, mysteriously dammed by some invisible barrier. It's enough to follow her slow, languid gestures, the movements of a professional sleeper, to guess that this young woman, who is apparently my contemporary, and who works as an underling in some office, is simply doing it to deceive, and is secretly developing in another dimension, another world, another present.

Jostled by a passenger, I let myself brush up against her. I am aware that she's quite obviously naked under her dress, and seems to me to be formed of a single curve of heavy, supple flesh, a single landscape of valleys and mountains. I am barely touching her, but she cambers herself so suggestively that I have to restrain myself from sliding my hands under her buttocks and penetrating her there, with her whole weight against my belly. All the woman in her pulverizes the three dimensions with an almost embarrassing insolence; her high breasts, her muscular rump, and above all, the exaggerated bulge of her sex under the cloth, so present that one feels it palpitating, voracious, always lying in wait, like some formidable beast of the caves. But the face of the young woman betrays nothing of this, as she dissimulates in her innermost depths. It expresses nothing save calm, immobility, and refusal. Whereas the others express, in body and face, brutality, sluttishness, and flab, she alone expresses distance and indifference, a waiting for nothing, exactly as if she had just come from some void endowed with climate, stripped of all, virgin of all identity, of all social definition, free of all ties, without profession, without sentiment,

without cowardice or nervous tics. Exactly as if she se-
creted an invisible, slow eddying of larval emotions, shadowy, savage, and steeped in the sap of fire that mounts as
high as her eyes. Once more, our eyes meet at close quarters. And for me only, in trust, she looks at me with an
almost toxic lucidity, kindling a true fire in the viscid flood
of her gaze. And in this brief look, charged with electricity, she causes a single spark to dance between tenderness
and desire, fear and bravado, defiance and equivocation—
the despair and joy of a second.

"Let's take a taxi," she says to me. "I would like, at least,
to be able to talk with you."

We find one easily, solidly lodged in a traffic jam which
does not seem about to break up. This gives us something
of a respite, which is above all what we desire.

Isolated from the crowd, cut off from the black and
white outside, the young woman loses nothing of her presence, her strangeness. No doubt about it, amidst a mass of
cadavers, more or less resuscitated for the purposes of the
cause, she actually resembles a living being, a resolutely
female creature who seems to live at the heart of herself,
with no care other than to take on life, her only employment that of living from day to day, with no other ambition than to survive—at once hypersensitive and uncaring,
tender and scornful, half drug, half poison, ironic and vul-
nerable, candid and perverse, indecent and reserved, passive and devouring, singularly steeped in her nocturnal,
luminous charm.

"Were you really born here?" I ask her.

She says "of course," giving me a smile at once fierce
and reassuring, a smile which reveals enough morbid
witchcraft, anguish, hunger, and thirst to freeze and burn
any interlocutor.

"What was your name before you were registered?" I
ask.

This is the first time that I have asked someone this question. The first time in fifteen years, since it was in 1984 that the Bureau of Civil Status replaced all names with numbers. But in this universe of figures, taxes, bills, and supervisory robots, numbers for people have always seemed quite sufficient to me, almost satisfying. Her alone it is impossible to designate by numbers.

"My name was Francine. And you?"

"Claude."

The word seems incongruous to me, obsolete, forgotten. I truly have the impression of talking about another person. I also have the impression that I am living the life of another in this moment, a parallel life, as incongruous as my name, effaced from the records, banned since long ago, buried.

"It's funny," Francine says to me. "I have had several lovers in my life. Not one of them asked what my name was. Nor did I ever ask them their names. I didn't call them anything. Besides, I had nothing to say to them."

"And to me?"

"To you, I could say almost everything. I knew this from the first minute."

Carefully, so as not to be seen in the driver's rearview mirror, she takes my hand, squeezes it, and then places it between her thighs, directly on the center of her animal warmth, on her naked sex, whose slow tide nibbles at my fingers.

I listen to her desire, she listens to my fingers. I drink her silence. It is more expressive than all the languages of the world. The warmth of her body releases more electricity than all the sunstrokes, wind, and thunder in the world. I am finally on vacation. I am on vacation at the edge of my desire; I turn my eye and head towards it. She is the abyss that I have always sought without ever believing that I would one day approach it. I recover it in love, softly, slowly, in secret. She is blending into my blood. Her sap enters my veins. I don't need to undress her, to lick her from the mouth to the ankles, to breach her, to know why I desire her with such passion. Her smell, like her look, or her overly raucous or muffled voice, defines her, denudes her, tells her story, but without ever explaining her. The details are unimportant; I know her essentials: with a singular evidence she evokes a creature come back from all without ever having left, a world that is larval and perfected, totally closed, impermeable to the surrounding stupidity, allergic to the universal grayness, a world which, at the beginning, was terror, living on its own inertia, on its fires, in its cocoon, a troubled and troubling world at once in fusion and fossilized, stammering and yet accomplished, made of tropics and chasms, indolence and silence. And this desire to slowly engulf myself in this world of night and swamps, to slip into it with my whole being, to be no longer anything but a continuous moan where to leave for a while one must make a good death, cooked on a slow fire, submerged, sucked up, mired, taken in the snare of this soft octopus of the abyssal depths. Only my hand, for the moment. Only my hand enters there, leaves reality, and Francine convulses around it, a spasm as insidious as a wave. She must have been inexplicably made to open and dissolve, as others were made to have children, work in offices, clean up, charge or pay cash. She is the perfection of the useless, the indefinite future, the embodiment of immediate presence and expectation without impatience, far from all connecting roads. She is the pleasure of subtracting oneself from the daily nightmare of three legal dimensions, to enter the subterranean dimension of a quasi-void where all must be reduced to shadows, a single slowness, an eternal groping.

"I want you," I tell her.

She answers with a groan cut short, hoarse, visceral. Her voice seems the exact reflection of her female presence. A voice almost without sonority, modulating its tones, very slow, too slow always, almost psalmodized. A voice made to moan in love, and then break, exhausted, breathless.

"How can you work in an office with such a voice?"

"At the office, I almost never speak. Not away from the office either, for that matter."

"What is it that you do in this office?"

"I type."

"Correspondence?"

"No. An advertising brochure for toothpaste. Always the same, besides, the last three years."

"They might have it printed. It would cost them less."

"It must be to provide work for me. Anyway, whether it's this or something else . . . I've done correspondence as well. It's always the same letter. Only the commas occasionally change."

"Do you have children?"

"A little girl. One day, she will be a secretary, like her mother. She will replace me. She will type up the toothpaste brochure that I will have left her, and which she will leave to her children. Nice, isn't it?"

It *is* nice. It is the first time that I have heard someone speak in order to say something. Someone who dares to take the risk to say something. It is the first time that I have seen a human being, a simple employee, seemingly accepting and agreeing so as to deceive, but hatching in secret a calm, underhanded revolt tinged with scorn and vitriol.

Suddenly, our taxi driver stops. We'd forgotten him. He asks us to get out and take another taxi.

"I am not a spy for the police, and I'm not especially

anxious to become one. But I can't say I like your conversation. I don't want trouble. The meter says twenty francs."

I pay him. We walk. We didn't cover more than two hundred yards in the hour we'd been in the taxi.

"I think I love you," Francine says before leaving me.

"I know I love you," I say to her.

I am just about to embrace her when a man approaches us.

"Your papers," he demands.

He examines them.

"You're not legitimate, either of you. What are you doing together on a public thoroughfare?"

I explain to him that the young woman was taken ill in the street, that I happened to pass by, and thought I was helping by accompanying her back to her place. He hesitates a moment, accepts my explanation, and tells us to separate. I acquiesce. Francine disappears into the tar-lined tunnel of her building. I do not even turn around to see it swallow her up, blending with the shadows that suit her so well.

July 20

Francine, Francine, Francine. I think only of her. I think of nothing else. She has inscribed her name upon a total void. For the first time in my life, I have something to think about.

The city is but a single labyrinth of microphones, recording machines, listening posts, intercoms, magneto-phones. The Office of Surveillance ferrets out all acts, all conversations, all writings, and all rendezvous, but one consolation is left me: they have not yet found a way to detect thoughts. Their cameras cannot yet penetrate me.

Within myself, I am writing endlessly to Francine, always talking to her, and no one will ever know of it.

July 30

The days pass, more monotonous than ever. The Center for Distribution of Time has for the past week been conducting a new experiment, unforeseen certainly, but quite simple: forcing us to spend the twelve working hours with ten minutes added on to each hour, and the twelve hours of leisure each shortened by ten minutes. Another source of profit for the State. The Popular Treasury is truly a bottomless cask. How could it be otherwise in a State which maintains millions of parasitic police, informers, functionaries, and others simply sworn to serve it?

August 3

On the first Thursday of the month, like every citizen, I am entitled to visit my close relatives—my mother, since none remain except her. She lives far from the center of town, on her modest Medium Superannuated pension. She is entitled to it for having worked all her life at the Central Office of Registry, spending only one day in prison; and for her total resignation, which has enabled her to come through it all without a single reprimand. Like her, like everyone, it will be my right to retire after forty-five; but I will receive no pension: I have been in prison more than once, I am down as an old offender in many offices, and my bills at the end of the year, which are never average, forbid me any hope of retiring one day with my M.S. pension. An absurd enough hope at any rate, with the pollution that has poisoned the city for more than thirty years: not much chance of living past forty.

August 5

There has been another arrest in the building where I
live: a man thirty years of age, accused of two extremely
grave offences. He was not working, doubtless living off
his legitimate mistress and, on the sly, was writing a ten-
dentious book which clearly had no chance of being ap-
proved by the Commission for Supervision of Writings.
In any case, no one who is not the rightful holder of a
governmental writer's card may write a single line, even
in secret. For one man, these amounted to numerous offences. An hour after being arrested by General Surveillance, he was arraigned before the tribunal of our residential block; I suppose he will be executed tomorrow
morning in one of the underground repression chambers.
Fortunately, he did not have occasion to show his manuscript to others. If they had read it, they doubtless would
have undergone the same fate. The State takes no chances
with writing; phrases, it seems, are what most surely poison minds.

August 9

Sometimes I tell myself I should have applied myself
and studied. But these regrets never last very long. The
most arduous studies can lead only to jobs as high functionaries in the police, as graded authorities, as promoters
in the pay of the Ministry of Profits, or as technicians
closely supervised by squads of technician police. All in
all, it's better in this world to stagnate as an underling of
the third category: less degrading, as yet.

And then, it's useless to delude oneself: even if I'd applied myself, I could never have finished each year among
the first ten in my class, which is the necessary condition

for not being eliminated at the end of the year, and being definitively dismissed from all schools. It's been thus since the great student confrontation of 1986, which nearly ignited a national uprising. A month later, the Ministry of Education became the Ministry of Repression, and entrusted to a pitiless Commission of Selection the task of reducing considerably the number of students. That is to say, for nearly fifteen years only elitist subjects, in which brilliant students alone have some chance of completing their studies, have been offered. The others have been swallowed up by the factories, the offices, or the innumerable supervisory ministries and centers, which sometimes leaves one the impression that half of the city's inhabitants are employed to spy on the other half.

As for the most inept, the ones one might have thought were irreclaimable, they are dumped in A.P., advertising production, which has increased considerably in scope these latter years: before 1975, advertising existed only in a tentative, larval stage, so to speak. Times have certainly changed. A recent survey has revealed that of fifteen million citizens, more than three million work in advertising. All this means is that there are many mediocrities, something one can see for oneself without delving into statistics.

But what is doubtless the most disconcerting about this is that in a completely functional world, oriented towards the useful and the utilitarian in scorn of the superfluous, advertising is for all intents and purposes operating in a void. It is intended for no end, without any idea of an actual product to be launched, with no design for inciting people to buy, or for increasing sales. It serves to support nothing. It is made up of empty phrases, meaningless slogans, gratuitous formulas, noisy assertions to no end. One does, in fact, have difficulty seeing what advertising could find to do in a city where commercial competition no longer exists, where objects of everyday use are reduced to very exact prototypes, products to a single brand. No customer could ever experience the fuss of choice: nothing is to be found on the market except the indispensable. Why this deluge of advertising, then? No doubt to brutalize the masses, to overwhelm and stuff them with words, with gray sounds and syllables. Nothing but words, never pictures. All graphic representation, all painting and photography have long since been banned in the city. Even the one monthly magazine in these last years— called *Promotion*—to which we are all obliged to subscribe, prints nothing but slogans, phrases suspended in the void, bubble words, exhausting, useless, dead. There'd be no need to obsess oneself over this if one were able to ignore the magazine *Promotion*, and never open it. But from time to time inspectors from Supervision of Reading carry out domicile raids and ask questions: one must be able to prove that one has read the official magazine if one wishes to avoid sanctions that can sometimes lead to prison. No doubt about it, all this is well organized; the trap is well laid. And how can you escape it? Impossible. I was born in this capital; I have a lifetime citizen's card, and it forbids me ever to change my city or my life. That, too, one must accept.

September 23

I had to wait before writing this. By playing around with time, they've ended by derailing it. Instead of going from the ninth of August to the tenth, we found ourselves in September 23rd. Time completely jumped the tracks overnight and, from high summer, we have passed to the threshold of autumn. This wasn't a serious inconvenience, I had nothing very particular to do at the end of

August and start of September and, as it had been hot for several days, the town seemed to be decomposing under a shroud of toxic stench, dust, detritus, marauding germs, and overheated gas.

Just the same, if the Center for Distribution of Time continues its experiments, they will end by jarring the planet loose from its orbit. That also would not seriously inconvenience me.

September 25

I see Francine nearly every day. We simply avoid seeing each other for too long, so as not to make ourselves conspicuous. We always meet in a compartment of the metro. During the rush hour, that is, between seven and midnight, the crowds are so dense, so thronging, that any supervision is nearly impossible. Then, after several stations, we each head separately for the exit and lose ourselves in the crowds on the great thoroughfares of the center. There too, in the seething mass of two-footed insects, supervision is difficult. As bit by bit the automobiles occupy maximum space in an eternal standstill, the pedestrians' only claim is sidewalks just wide enough for a couple of average weight. In this swarming grayness, it's difficult to tell who is with whom. When, by chance (and this has happened), an inspector approaches me and demands my papers, Francine ignores me and allows herself to be carried away by the current of passersby. And I do the same when it's her they're interrogating. One mustn't forget that we have already been seen in front of her place. We may already be pegged, suspected, on the books as possible offenders with a record. And the whole city is in fact one gigantic eye, whose sole desire is to catch us in the act.

In the subway, I am content to sink into the vertigo

which her presence and smell deepen; in the street, without ever touching her, I talk with her. And from pavement to pavement, from street to street, I learn things, I learn to understand, I learn why I am drawn to her.

Francine had a father who must have spoken with her and told her things when she was still very young. He was a professor of history. Of contemporary history only, of course, since no one is allowed to make the slightest allusion to the history of the world prior to 1980. But he was not one to be duped. He had pursued his studies in the 60's; he knew the history of the world and the past, of the planet and forgotten worlds. And he had forgotten none of this pernicious information. Even if he didn't so much as mention it to his students, he doubtless talked to his daughter about it. Impossible to insert the least subversive allusion in a lecture: the courses were always audited by a cultural inspector, recorded, sifted, filtered, reexamined, and kept under surveillance by the Mental Espionage agency.

"I loved him very much," Francine told me today. "He was arrested one morning and executed that evening. He dared to speak before a hundred students or so of a strike which broke out in a factory in 1992, and was finally settled by troops firing point-blank. It seems that this was one of the last recorded attempts at collective revolt."

"Careful, we're being followed. Go on ahead without me," I say to Francine.

September 26

We're barely out of the subway when Francine resumes her conversation, just as if she had been merely interrupted by a car's horn.

"He was a human being, not an employee. The only

human being I ever met. He loved me, too. He often told me not to rebel, that it was useless: I'd simply be executed. But he also told me not to accept this world, that I must be aware and refuse to resign myself to it. And you, who taught you to despise it?"

"I don't know. I have always been indifferent to it all. I have always detested men. Men and their enterprises, like so many pretentious beavers."

"Just how old are you?"

"I was born in 1969, I'm thirty years old."

"At least you know what it was like before 1980."

"Very vaguely. I don't remember much. I know that the world was already going rather badly in 1970. And you got the feeling that it would get even worse."

"It's funny, you know almost nothing, but you know what's essential. It's a pity that you didn't know my father. Perhaps you'll join him one day, if you end like him in the common grave of criminals."

"No. I'm too much of a coward for that."

September 27

I have always been indifferent, that's true. I have never gone so far as to revolt. Useless: there are too many of them and, above all, they are too well organized. But I have always been lucid. I have never accepted this world. I have always known. Only now, since I have known Francine, something more violent is slowly growing in me. Something which is no longer indifference or contempt. A certain revolt at the idea of being confined with her, in the same universe with her, on the same level of existence, and strictly separated from her by the barriers of this same universe. A certain latent revolt, sly, continuous. Lucky for me I'm a coward, or I would feel almost capable of commiting a senseless act, whatever it might be, at the cost of whatever punishment.

It's 11 P.M. I am on the court of my Tennis Club, where I'm obliged to perform my athletic duty every day. During the day, I'm an employee of the pen; nights, an employee of the racket.

Before, when I found myself playing here without pleasure or verve, I'd say to myself that it was no different elsewhere. Now it disgusts me to be here; I'd like to be in a wilderness of sheets with Francine, to lose myself in that desert, lie low there with no hope of finding the way out, the end, civilization.

But I am here, on an indoor court, across from the partner who has been assigned to me this evening. A stranger as always, always a different stranger, so that no non-athletic relationship may form. She has the dull complexion, the frigid appearance, the bovine calm and bearing of women who have only known the frustrations of the office and olympic joys. Her face is expressionless as a tennis ball, almost as round, with two unseeing eyes, eyes which are merely holes for observing the balls coming towards her, and balls returned. Neither does she have any figure. Nothing but two overly solid legs, two overly muscular arms. No sex, no breasts, no ass—these aren't needed in the office or on the court. Just by her arrogant air, one guesses that she must be a section head in an important office. Just by her way of holding her tin of tennis balls, one feels that she has been playing with conviction on the courts since childhood. She's a professional at work and sports, and nothing else. She seems so perfectly conditioned that I wonder if, after a day of labor and sport, she isn't disassembled and stored in a cupboard for the next day. I hate her. She has that stunned, distant air of simplex people with important responsibilities, who are constantly chalking up points, who know the law and karate—people with clout and backhands, who give nothing aside from orders, never think, and are ceaselessly active, sure of themselves, aware of being steeped in the brine of truth, faith, justice, morality, and dignity. I hate her more than the planet, or as much. To have Francine before me, I would not hesitate to kill this partner of mine. And I don't even have the consolation of saying to myself, "well, if I can't kill her, I can at least execute her in three sets." It is she who will beat me, without giving me a sporting chance: I've known this since the first volley.

Never have I felt so totally beyond the pale as at this precise moment. I feel myself as alien to this decor, to this evening and this game of mentally arrested adults, to this Earth-thing in her folk costume, to this whole complex conspiracy of boredom and leisure, as strange to all this as if I had always lived millions of miles removed from this planet, and had only just now been catapulted into it without a manual, without anything to do, without warning, and without means of defending myself, of fleeing, or explaining myself.

Francine, or terror. That is perhaps why she strikes and moves me with the force of an invisible tide. Everything in her expresses the panic of living a permanent nightmare, the horror of having nothing else to live, the silent revolt at having one day to pass from this cluttered, noisy void to a shadowy, unpopulated void. Francine and her sleepwalker's tread, that measures out her despair without a cry or lament, all her claws sheathed, flayed yet calm, ironic and lost, stranger to all, misplaced in this time and space, wandering, unnecessary, and useless.

It is perhaps for this reason that I feel the desire to shatter in pieces the dismal playing-machine that moves before me: to determine if, before dying, some vague glimmer of fear or disquiet might not shadow her mummified cow's gaze. But it's useless to speculate: one would see nothing at all there. Perhaps some slight irritation at the thought of dying before having finished a game that was hers, hands down; a reaction of anger at being forced to quit. Dying, for her, must be nothing more than the end of a set, or at most, of the match. She would be placed in a coffin stamped with the arms of the club, with her racket held between her hands like a giant crucifix, and all the players, in white jerseys and mourning shorts, would follow her remains. Graveside speakers would recall the grace of her forehand, the efficacy of her backhand, the force of her service, and the salutary dryness of her interventions at the net; they would also recall that she was the faithful companion of a man whom she had met during a volley, and that they had gone on to produce numerous little balls of their own. They might even shed a tear over her death on the court of honor, in the heat of action after a busy day well spent. And God, wiping away a tear, would no doubt grant her the blessing of returning to Earth to complete her set.

Anyway, I have just lost the first two sets, as I foresaw. We're starting on the third.

I no longer know very well where I am. I no longer have the faintest idea what I am doing on this wooden surface, my hand soldered to a racket which seems as heavy as lead, my eyes blurry, and my mind elsewhere, my body mechanically sweeping the area with volleys, backhands, and drives, an area onto which I'd just like to collapse, with one howl of rage and panic. Love and hate. Aside from these, I feel nothing. And I experience no subtler feelings. Between these two poles, there is no space for compromise. I love a woman who is always absent, and yet so singularly, ceaselessly present. As for the rest, the planet and all its furnishings, taken piecemeal or in bulk, with its decor and its accessories, I hate it.

And little by little, as I might have feared, things are coming into focus, and crystallizing. I secretly feel a nucleus of genuine coldness and scorn forming inside me, taking me all in, coagulating as if I were simply water seized with frost. All that still burns in me is my gaze, filled with vitriol; it makes a hole in my sockets. So nakedly do I feel it, curetted by so dolorous a lucidity that I could almost swear that my eyes have usurped the rest of my face. And this look has just attached itself to the one living prey that moves in my range of action: my partner.

A symbol, truly. An ideal mark to aim at, a symbolic résumé of everything and nothing; and now it is as if I were examining her through a lens, swollen with all the terrifying banality that she secretes; heavy with her lack of charm and grace, pregnant with the millions of stupid things she has said, with all that she will say before the end of her time; inflated with pretention and male assertiveness. My partner, this one or another, this one, as it turns out, interchangeable, colorless, and odorless like the majority of female bipeds, neither beautiful nor ugly, not this, not that, pasteurized, platitudinized, mineralized, bureaucratized, monopolized, always between two mediocre averages, neck-deep in moderation, steeped in convention up to their assholes, impossible to define unless they're holding a racket, a vacuum cleaner, a lampstand, a pencil, or a microphone. Suddenly, I realize that I am condemned to meet, by the thousands, everywhere, endlessly, the women of this breed without breeding or femininity, without expression and without sap; that some of them will single me out, demanding money and charge accounts, will require my papers or my blood; that others will be my neighbors, my relatives, my family, my doctors, my superiors or my subordinates, my investigators or my prison guards, while Francine will doubtless always be domiciled elsewhere, far from me, half lost, and always found again, only to be lost again. At that moment, for the first time in longer than I can remember, a feeling of genuine revolt rises in me. And what can one do with it when all one has is a racket and a ball?

My partner has just returned a shot, too high and weak, which drops around a yard from the net. From the base line where I am, I plunge towards the net; I summon up a supreme effort and smash the ball just at the height of its bounce. It's what is called a sure point, a shot one can place anywhere with power, impossible to return. But I have no intention of placing this shot and winning the point. It's the head of my partner I'm aiming at in a savage, ultimate volley, with all the force of a well-prepared forehand. The ball in fact flies almost horizontally, catapulted at the neck of my partner, who skillfully dodges the cotton meteor.

It was not only the gloomy mug of my partner that I wished to hit and disfigure; it was the women, the men, the city, the state, the schedules, the days, the police, money, the nights, the world, the sky, the constraints, everything that characterizes the life of the whole planet. But, by a mere one or two inches, I missed my target.

"*Out,*" my partner remarks with some perspicacity.

She smiles, relieved. I've missed an easy point on a ball which was a serious mistake on her part. If I'd gotten the point, her evening would have been marred.

Out, in fact. Fifteen love in her favor. But I'm the one who's out, much more so than the ball.

September 30

"You're going to end up in prison," Francine assures me when I tell her what happened last night.

"I am in prison," I tell her. "Without you, I am constantly incarcerated."

"Me too—I think of you all the time."

"I don't think we can stand it any longer. We will simply have to find a way of making love."

She smiles. It is just the news that she wanted to tell me. We're going to be able to legally spend a night together, one night at least. One of her friends has become the legitimate mistress of a high functionary in Sexual Affairs. She is going to try to get her a forged adultery card.

I listen to her, and I have the sensation that the sidewalk is becoming an immense puddle of tar in which I am sinking up to the knees.

October 4

What happened one October 3rd between 1980 and 1999? One may well ask oneself this. Doubtless an event the government is intent on utterly effacing. And to prevent any risk of any commemoration whatever, the Center for Distribution of Time regularly suppresses, every year, the third of October. I have already attempted to find out what might have happened on this day. A proletarian strike? A failed *coup d'état*? A massive execution? No one knows, or no one dares answer this question.

October 6

I was unable to go out. For a reason which neither the

Radio nor the *Quotidian* have revealed to me, the Central
Office of Orders and Prohibitions has banned access to
this day to pedestrians. Another ten hours of work at the
office which I will have to make up.

October 10

Yet another week which will be as monotonous to live
as the others, but more rich in bother. It must in fact be
unfolding under the aegis of the Ministry of Profits, and is
wholly devoted to compulsory purchase. Each inhabitant
must, on each day of this week, acquiesce in one or more
purchases totaling not less than one hundred francs; food
and household items don't count.

The city has never been more sinister than on this occasion. It's all one can do to make one's way through the
soft mass of pedestrians who have invaded the sidewalks
in search of a buy, between the cars that desperately seek
where to avoid the flux and reflux of subway users. In the
vicinity of the great stores that have piled in their windows veritable avalanches of noisily advertised eyesores,
cordons of commercial police and gigantic doormen brutally regulate the traffic of buyers, with blows and orders,
shoving and interdiction. The fracas of injunctions and
slogans brayed out by the sales loudspeakers blends with
the uproar of traffic. And, to punctuate the gloomy mass
delirium, pale placards attached at all levels everywhere
announce the stupidest slogans: "Step right in, it's more
expensive here than across the street," "You know the inspectors will see you when you buy here," "Reluctant buyers beware," "To buy at a high price is to survive at bar-
gain rates," "Time is money: spend it all before it's too
late."

Even the sky is gray this morning, like the street, the

complexions and suits of the passersby, the store windows and the objects on display: as if the entire city is one great advertisement to the glory of a week in gray. As for the air, it is so filthy that one finally asks oneself whether the microbes are not visible to the naked eye, so heavy and glaucous that one is astonished at being able to advance through it more easily than under water. As often in this season, it is neither hot nor cold, good nor bad weather. It's nothing: there is no climate, no temperature, no air, no sky. One might believe oneself in a vast room, tepidly heated by a multitude of radiators which give off smoke, fumes of petrol and carbonic gas, soot and stench through all the holes in their valves.

In every street, there are men from the Purchase Supervision Brigade. One must prove to them, with bill and package as evidence, that one has in fact made a purchase, sometime during the day before 7 P.M., of at least one hundred francs. I am very anxious not to know exactly what penalty any infraction of this law entails.

This week will also witness the triumph of advertising, not only of that kind with an end in view, but also of that which delights in absurd slogans, scattered broadcasts for nothing. To second the brayings of the loudspeakers and the silent cries of the posters, gangs of hucksters distribute brochures which it is out of the question to refuse or carelessly discard. I already have an armful, and am taking on others in a pitiless rhythm. Most of them brag about the prestige of products which have never existed, vindicate imaginary brands, make lying offers which don't stand up, or vilify competing brands which, quite often, don't exist either. In other words, if one finds almost nothing on this market, or only the absolute minimum, publicity offers an impressive sampling of whatever utopia it may be: fountain pens which last only an hour, tins of milk with two babies to try it on, razor blades which will last for over ten years, toothpastes which guarantee your skeleton a dazzling smile, lingerie which dissolves the first time you wash it, detachable items which make irreparable holes in your clothing, cheeses impregnated with deodorants, typewriters which never make mistakes, quick energy drinks for harassed pedestrians, clocks which give you the time a year ahead, everything, in fact, for everyone.

Well, after long indecision I finished by buying a supply of socks. These are always useful, at least if I don't lose my feet before the end of the month.

October 15

Since there is no such thing as unemployment, since work is obligatory for all those who are not beneficiaries of the official retirement pension, it was indeed necessary to create new jobs. The Ministry of Distribution of Daily Work does not hesitate, in cases of poverty, to impose strictly useless jobs, conceived simply to absorb personnel. That is why, this morning, the *Quotidian* is announcing the formation of a new municipal service: the punching of subway tickets, which will relegate to that underground world several thousand currently available workers. A peculiarly weird idea: subway tickets have, for a long time, been obtained and punched automatically. No matter. At each station there will be a puncher to make a second hole in them. Sometimes I ask myself if the anonymous high officials of the State don't possess a sense of black humor, and if the city is not their collective butt. How can one know? How can one judge or suspect them? No one has ever seen their faces, no one has ever approached them, no one speaks of them, and their profiles do not even appear symbolically on banknotes, stamps, or Camembert wrappers.

October 18

I finally received this morning the ticket which I had requested four months ago, to attend a performance of *The Employee*, the only play that may currently be seen. Besides, there is only one theater in the entire city, the Scenic Palace, where this play has been running for ten years.

I got away from it, but I cannot get over it. People must truly be empty shells, devitalized and shiftless, completely bloodless, to put up with a spectacle of this sort. It takes more than six hours, and relates at leisure—dead in its tracks—the interminable ascension of an employee in Contributions who rises from the rank of a subordinate of the first category to that of an assistant supervisor. Every scene takes place in a single office setting, where virtually speechless characters slowly rot, fossilized, conditioned, eroded, endowed with a language which is the exact and legal reflection of the daily life of their employment. In fact, one could swear that the theater was built next to an office of Contributions, that a partition had been removed, and that for ten years the spectators had paid very high prices to surfeit their gaze on a reality in strict conformity with the most threadbare banality. And everyone stands for it, no one murmurs the least word of criticism, no one ever gives a sign of weariness. They even applaud at the end. They follow with close attention, they accept it, they participate.

I alone, after two hours, got up and headed for the exit. I didn't get that far, nabbed quietly in the corridor by two inspectors of leisure.

"Are you leaving the theater?" one of the men courteously inquired.

"Well, I . . ."

"Does the play not meet with your approval? You have

some criticism to make? Does it bore you? Do you really
want your name to go into the Protestors' Files?"

I say no, certainly not, I don't think so, I don't really
want that at all. And I return to my seat.

Several years ago, I left a theater one day, stating that
the film displeased me. This got me a month in prison,
and a five thousand franc surtax for contestation. I know
this music. It has one note, a trifle high for my taste.

October 20

It is the day for the weekly visit of my lawful mistress.
After having made love, with as much passion as if we
were taking a foot bath, we are silent and awkward with
each other. As we truly have nothing to say to each other,
we go for a drink to the "492," the one café on 492nd
Street where I'm domiciled. We have no choice in the
matter: as a resident of this street, I am forbidden to go
elsewhere.

In any case, "elsewhere" no longer means a thing. Elsewhere and everywhere, it's the same: all the cafés have
exactly the same dimensions and decor, and they serve
the same drinks without alcohol, without tang, and without taste.

"Two sodas," orders my lawful mistress. "You have verbena?"

They do.

"Two verbenas, then."

What luck, they have verbena. And what luck to be able
to consume it in this establishment adorned with great
mirrors which reflect back and forth like a mournful echo
a labyrinth of mirrors, dirty plaster, befuddled customers,
and muffled conversations which cannot escape the microphones pegged in each table, or the supervisors of con-

versation who circulate endlessly through the consumers' ranks.

I study my lawful mistress. I try to gaze at her impassively, without betraying my desire to wring her neck when I think that I am here with her and do not even know where Francine might be. I scrutinize and judge her. She is nothing. She is neither my friend, nor my favorite perversion, nor my preferred kind of face; she is not my ideal washerwoman, nor my refuge, nor my truth, nor even the mother of my child. She is nothing but the first salesgirl I slept with more than three times, which made it legitimate according to a pitiless law that admits of no exceptions. More than three times, enough to snare me, while the first time sufficed and satiated me. I try to comprehend how she could have seduced me, and I no longer see, exactly. No doubt it was her body, her flat stomach and her well-proportioned breasts, her perfect buttocks, a certain kind of figure, with some elegance. Nothing less, but nothing more. Aside from these rather tempting curves, there is nothing: no intelligence, a nothing sensibility, a stupid candor, a sulky and depressed character, a face without interest, unseeing, unsmiling, without expression other than application and professional conscientiousness. In short, a woman of our time.

"What are you thinking about?" she asks me, since this question is one of the few within her imaginative range.

"I was thinking about you."

My answer disconcerts her, and she does not answer. Born of salespeople degraded by their circumstances, she has difficulty understanding phrases that do not directly refer to sale or purchase.

"The verbena's very good here," she says to me.

Succulent, one might say, succulent. And so much in harmony with this place, these consumers, and this ambiance, this couple that we form. This verbena tastes like my life: insipid, sweetish, tepid. And the same aftertaste of latent nausea.

October 25

For more than a week now I have been waiting for Francine in vain in the subway, at the hour we fixed as our permanent rendezvous. No one has come for so long. I'm not overly disturbed by it. There again, I am without illusions. There are so many imponderables that may enter the game at any second.

Only this evening do I find her again, unchanged, still as intimate, with an inner light, indolent, feverish.

"I thought you were in prison," I tell her.

"I nearly was."

I observe that it did not occur to me for an instant to doubt her. To think that she had withdrawn, was playing games, or had suddenly gotten cold feet. It seems clear to me that these feints, these little flights, could only belong to a past forever forgotten, forever passed.

"I nearly was," Francine repeats. "Eight days ago, I received a notice from the Office of Orders and Prohibitions. I was expressly forbidden to leave my place for a week."

"Under what pretext?"

"Not a word of explanation. Simply an order."

"You think we've been discovered?"

She doesn't know, she doesn't think so.

But who can know? In any case, it's useless to harbor too many illusions: in this world, there is nothing to inspire long-term hopes. Only a few fires vaguely kindled in secret, ruses performed at enormous risk. And the instant that, from the depths of the daily nightmare, there surges a moment of exaltation, a reason for hoping, the shadow of a decree, a law lies in wait to fall on it, to completely do away with it. Formerly, there were three worlds in the reality of everyday: that of metaphysical horror, which is ever present and has never varied; that of the aberrant complexities of the everyday; and that of the innumerable diversions which enabled one to stand it. This world of diversions has long since disappeared. The authorities have decided that it is useless, unprofitable, and too attractive to be legal. The moments of forgetfulness or relaxation have been withdrawn from us as easily as a rug from under our feet. These moments could never be quite real where we are, wedged between two parallels of terror. Only the minutes of fear and boredom, of torture and anxiety are real, tangible, recorded, official.

And if they had in fact discovered us, and had decided to secretly sabotage our adventure without coming down on us officially, without throwing us in prison or separating us by force or by jurisdiction? Who knows? I was told as a fact one day that there has always existed an Office for Tracking Down Consolations, the sole purpose of which is to relentlessly ferret out the slightest moments of release, and to destroy them like bubbles. Perhaps this is true? Perhaps this invisible bureau actually exists, anonymous, underground, all powerful. This would not surprise me in the least.

"What are we going to do?" Francine asks me.

"Nothing. Continue to see each other. We shall see."

November 2

Nothing, always nothing.

We see each other nearly every day, and nothing has happened to us. There hasn't been the slightest penalty imposed on us; no office takes the least bit of interest in us.

November 4

It was just nine o'clock when I was summoned by my section chief at the firm where I work.

"I have received a note concerning you," he informed me. "You are going to be transferred."

I felt the floor falling away from beneath my feet. I sat down. I felt the chair also become a patch of quicksand. I could feel myself liquefying, blending with the substance of the chair. You are going to be transferred. Me, transferred? We had then, Francine and I, been discovered as I'd feared. And now I was being underhandedly transferred, relegated, no doubt, to the one branch of this firm, to the annex of offices situated ten kilometers from the center of the city. Which meant that never again would I be able to find Francine on the subway line which both of us used every evening at the same hour. They had detected our point of junction, and with derisive ease, a smudge of the thumb, they had erased it. As simple as that.

"Don't you feel well?" the section chief inquired.

I stammered out that I felt fine.

"Instead of working at the third level, starting from next week you will work at the fourth. And everybody in your office will be demoted by one step."

Was that all? That was all. Nothing but that? Nothing but that. It took me over two hours to recover from the shock.

November 7

Yesterday, suddenly, at ten o'clock, a break in time.

Several weeks had passed since we had had an incident

of this kind, an incident which, besides, is extremely commonplace.

It always happens in the same way, exactly like a power failure. I was about to calibrate page eight; I had counted 21,564 punctuation marks, when suddenly nothing, a black hole, and a few seconds later I was looking at page eight again, but could not remember that I had reached 21,564. It was a day later, ten minutes past three.

The same evening, I meet Francine in the subway. And suddenly I feel a paralyzing sense of disquiet, hardly less overwhelming than this afternoon, or yesterday. I tell Francine to wait for me inside the exit.

"The adultery card which you were supposed to get. . . . At least they didn't give it to you yesterday?"

"Not yet," Francine says.

I breathe more regularly, and regain some calmness of manner.

"What's the matter?" Francine asks.

"Imagine if you had received the card yesterday. It would have been valid only for that day. In other words, it would have been wasted because there was a break in time that lasted more than twenty-four hours."

"You don't suppose that the Center thought this up simply to prevent us from making love?"

"I don't know. I no longer know. I wouldn't put anything past them."

"Even to lose the income of a day of work from millions of people?"

She has a point. I sometimes have the impression that I am breaking down. And I don't even have the resource of revealing my condition to the official company doctor, during his next visit at the end of the month. If he learns that my nerves are going, he will report me to the Bureau of Depressions, which will transfer my file to Mental Control. There, they will seek to find out why I am breaking down. And there's no point in doubting it: they will find out very quickly. And it won't be a clinic I'll find myself in, but a prison cell.

November 11

Today is a day off. The only we get aside from Christmas.

Christmas, because great emphasis is laid on religion these days. It is imposed on everyone, even if one's an atheist, something one must hide with care. And every day at the stroke of eleven to undergo the company mass is not the least tedious feature of a working day. There can be no question of skipping it, of listening inattentively, or of speaking of it with any disrespect. C.P. (Christian Power) has made the law for nearly twenty years; it controls all the bureaus, holds sway over all the ministries, and watches over every soul; it directs the police, and it is its blood with which the subterranean brain of the city is nourished.

On the other hand, November 11th commemorates a much obscurer event. It seems that this date is that of the end of a war. As for knowing exactly which. . . . A lost war in a lost past. I seem to remember that my father spoke of it occasionally, but war was his *bête noire*, his principal subject of conversation: you might have thought that wars were ready-made, and broke out every week then.

Abolished, obsolete notion. With whom could we have a war, since we are living in a sealed vessel, cut off from everything? The word "foreign" has become totally foreign to us.

Perhaps to give us some idea of what war represented, the radio broadcasts throughout the day of November 11th a continuous uproar of noises of combat, bombardments, and explosions. I don't know whether it was dangerous, but it certainly seems to have been noisy. And extremely monotonous.

November 14

What the offices tolerate with difficulty is lateness.

No doubt I have a sense of the hour, but I have never had a sense of the minute, or even of the quarter hour. Thus it happens that I arrive late for work. And each minute of lateness costs me dear: to be precise, fifty francs for the first time in the month, one hundred francs the second time, and so on. It's these little details that are the last straw for a salary already seriously reduced by various other more or less freakish impositions, but all legal and legalized. For me personally, each minute of lateness costs twice the official tariff. It is in fact five years now that I've had a red file in the central files at the Office of Schedules. That of permanent offenders. In addition to monthly fines, this means that I have to "voluntarily" contribute at the end of the year to the Lateness Allocations Treasury. Nothing is lost these days, least of all lost time.

November 20

The annual Day of Death falls on a Tuesday this year. It is not a day off, but it has its importance, its obsessive presence, for everything on this day revolves around death. Whether it is in our offices or in our apartments, in the hallways or in the streets, we are constantly at the mercy of the representatives of death who methodically traverse the city from neighborhood to neighborhood, according to a vast, planned "rake-off" which leaves nothing to chance, and no one outside its reach. Like death itself, in fact, it's quite regular. And like death, its representatives are there to remind us, at least once a year, that we are not forgotten. Some quietly buttonhole us in order to take our exact measurements. Others to check on our mortuary installments, which we have to pay all our lives, and which assure us, as it were, of the one future which is inexorably reserved for us: a decent burial, a coffin guaranteed to be comfortable, and a place in the sun of the void, in a region said to be picturesque and free of pollution. Putting it another way, these municipal employees represent a product which we have no chance of refusing. Impossible anyway: here, death costs the same for everyone, a trifle overpriced, but unless one can prove one's immortality it's impossible to avoid this tax.

But all this ado no longer really troubles anyone, aside from a few professional worriers like myself. Death, for more than fifteen years, no longer presents itself as a subject for panic or horror. Life, death, what's the difference? Everyday life seems as dreary as certain death. One is inured to the idea; there's not much to regret in leaving this planet. One doesn't lose much in a world where one possesses nothing. One accepts death as one accepts the constant surveillance, the ever-waiting trap of prison, the ever-present menace of capital execution, the monotonous work in a vacuum, the lack of all freedom, and the invading presence of rapacious and repressive laws.

And in any case, the neo-Christian religion has conditioned us; it has imposed its law by dint of argument, commentary, and morbid propaganda. Religion teaches us, in fact, that death is after all nothingness, the long rest to

which we're all entitled after a life of forced labor, an
ideal repose without constraints, without police, contributions, or daily torture. Religion also teaches us to live our
lives patiently, since, with only a few exceptions, they do
not last much more than forty years—whether we like it
or not. And, it promises, the worst is yet to come, beyond
our hopes: with increasing pollution, the average life-span
will soon drop to thirty years.

For twenty-four hours, the Radio inundates us with slogans for death, slogans which the *Quotidian* inflicts on us
in print. Not all resemble each other, but they all belong
to the same family, in mourning for all hope. "To die is to
smile a little." "He who is dead will not die." "One dead
man is worth two living men." "Despair doesn't pay the
bill." "Why believe in life when only death believes in
you!" "To be born is to be dead." "An hour of death will
make up for twenty years of work." "He who dies needs
no dinner." "Well-lived life profits no one." "It's in the
grave that one stops working." "United we die." "Never
die tomorrow if you can do it today." "Never mind about
dying in time, one must rot in time." "It's in dying every
day that one becomes moribund." "Death helps you endure poverty."

And the statistics released by the *Quotidian* state even
more emphatically that all hopes are permissible. Everything is going better and better. The mortality rate for
1999 is sharply up from that of 1998. There are more than
one hundred capital punishments daily, more traffic acci-
dents than ever, a steady rise in deaths from pollution, a
sharp recrudescence of other mortal illnesses, and a very
satisfactory number of suicides. In short, all is well.

Everything is going so well in this superbly organized
nightmare that sometimes I ask myself why I'm so afraid

of dying. I must be a true coward. Really hopeless. Morbidly attached to life. Might as well admit it: I'm abnormal.

Francine belongs to the same breed as myself. Probably a breed which is on the way to extinction. This may be why she has so vividly expressed her fears, whenever I see her.

"I'm afraid, Claude, afraid all the time. They're all crazy. This life terrifies me, but death terrifies me even more."

I am not able even to hold Francine against me, to enter her body with mine to prove to her that life is sometimes an easy, fascinating death, slow and in full possession of itself.

She undeniably has the air of being terrorized. Nothing more nor less, but how can I believe it? In a compact mob of employees functioning at 100 percent capacity in resigned buggery, I met a young woman who seemed to have no other social *raison d'etre* than calm, everyday dread. No one had ever given me such an impression of having never done anything, of being as absolutely allergic to all action, of being without definite employment, without a past as much as without a future. Of being an eternal and useless, indefinite present. And the most disquieting thing about her is to feel that the covered fire that burns within her forever burns in vain, all the more baleful for that; even her lupine thirst and hunger are for no end, running free in an inward world that can only be a blind road which nothing can reach, where no one will ever pass.

Who are you? I am constantly desirous of asking her this question, even when I know her so well, so much better than the armored reality that surrounds me on all sides. A mirage? A human animal? A humanoid animal? A voracious mineral? A thinking vegetable? A somber gleam made woman? A dead person come back to life, or a living person born in death? But whatever the answer is, if there is one to this futile question, even if I am never to live a single night with her, I will always retain my certainty that it would have been as gentle as cruelty, pure as troubled water, indecent as terror, hard as mud, indolent as sleep, heavy as absence, darkling and sweet as poison, heavenly life-sucking and deadly magical, horribly beautiful, and a terrifying relief.

"I want you," she murmurs. "I'd like to leave with you. Escape."

To leave here, to escape: these are indeed words which no longer mean anything. By train, as by car, leaving the city entails visas, official authorizations that there is no chance of our obtaining. And without papers we won't get far. And even if we managed to escape this urban trap, they'd soon find us. And the law hardly makes exceptions for attempted breakouts: it means death.

It remains to be seen whether it would not be better to live a few days with her and then die, than to drag out another ten years or so in this gigantic concrete office.

November 25

This year, as every year in the last week of November, the Exhibition of Daily Work opened. The same morning, each inhabitant receives by mail an admission ticket. It is offered, free of charge, by the Ministry of Compulsory Leisure. This means that one has to attend the Exhibition, under penalty of a fine.

To visit it is to wander for several hours through a maze of offices. Most of the stands are re-creations, astoundingly realistic, of various types of office. Thus, one passes

from a commercial messenger service to a model accounting office, from an expediter's service to a managerial
office, from an entry hall to a cloakroom. One admires
attractive showcase displays of pencils and typewriters,
note pads and carbon paper, balls of string and labels,
clasps, and file boxes. The viewers go there as they go to
work, apathetic, silent, thick witted, befuddled. And if
they have an uncomplimentary remark to make, they know
better than to say it.

At the exit, the big Suggestion Box gives the tone of the
visitors' apathy, the general discretion. Everything is always perfect, admirably presented, very interesting, instructive, even better than last year. Never the slightest
disobliging remark, never a snide allusion, no criticism or
persiflage.

November 28

And yet, every day there are acts of rebellion, of isolated
insubordination. They are carefully hushed up, but they
happen. I suppose the witnesses of such acts are immediately thrown in jail.

Despite everything, there are leaks from time to time.
Thus today, at the office, one of my colleagues spoke to
me in veiled allusions of an incident that took place this
week. Exasperated by the daily rush-hour traffic jams, a
driver managed to extricate his car, and ram it full speed
into one of the annex offices of Directed Contributions.
The resultant fire caused lots of damage.

When one thinks about it, the car is the one weapon
that man has at his disposal. A dangerous one, as has been
proved on the highways. But is it conceivable?—a mass
action undertaken by all drivers? It's quite unlikely. In
general, they cling to their cars as to their most cherished

possession; every morning and every night, they dutifully gulp down the tranquilizers prescribed by Highway Security. This, plus their natural degradation, has made them a docile flock, easy to lead.

December 2

And now another year is nearly over.

The distance between the cradle and the grave diminishes. And before we know it, in another month we'll be in the year 2000.

For myself personally, one question bothers, dogs, haunts me: Will I make love with Francine in the twentieth or twenty-first century?

As for the rest of the planet, its metaphysics and its history, it can go cook an egg.

December 5

To celebrate the dignified entry of the planet into the twenty-first century, the Center for Distribution of Time intends to add a December 32nd to the month, unique in the annals of history. It will be considered a day off, and will serve as a true inauguration of the century to come.

To make up for this day, the Center proposes, from tomorrow on, to have days of twenty-three hours only.

December 6

One can only believe that the formula of the twenty-three hour day is not going as planned.

In all the western districts of the city it was night, while day was in full swing in all the others, except for the center, where people underwent an alternation of night and day that at certain moments was as rapid as their blinking at it.

The Ministry of Returns protested officially against these time disturbances which could not but have a harmful effect on work.

December 7

The Center for Distribution of Time is to be credited with having taken a rather original initiative, but it does not seem as if this initiative was very successful.

Time has been stabilized, of course: night followed day very normally after a classic dawn, and even a twilight at the close of afternoon, but the temporal distortions have had an unforeseen, even unforeseeable consequence: everything to do with the complexities of electromagnetic equipment has been in a state of total blackout since midnight. The Radio is off the air. The television screens are blank. The loudspeakers are mute. The microphones and surveillance intercoms are useless.

No one has taken advantage of it, or seems even to think of it, but there is no longer any way of bugging private conversations, no way of spying on citizens through the walls, floors, and ceilings.

On the other hand, the committees of repression and surveillance bureaus must be aware of this. If only they could declare war on the Center for Distribution of Time, take arms, and kill each other to the last man.

December 8

If there were something like a weather bureau for time, it would give a completely reassuring report: "Time is stable and well regulated, divided into hours of sixty minutes, each containing sixty seconds." But this could never be more than appearance. A bulletin too polite to be honest. In reality, it seems that there have been dissimilar chain reactions. Each day has its unexpected event. Today's may well stupefy all those who have always believed in the stability and permanence of civilization.

It's dreamlike: everything which is made of plastic material has evaporated in space and time. Or more exactly, this matter has dissolved in space because of time. There is not the slightest trace of it left anywhere, exactly as if the century had inexplicably been situated before the invention of plastic.

The shock was all the more spectacular in that most of our everyday objects are made of plastic: dustbins, wardrobes, boxes, bottles, and household devices. That is to say, fifteen million inhabitants spent the entire day collecting tons of contents strewn on the ground, sponging floors clean, clearing away and arranging the huge avalanche of things and products hurled to earth, on the pavements and in apartments, in cellars and offices, everywhere, at all levels, as if a formless lava had burst through millions of barriers.

All this begins to excite me intensely. What does tomorrow hold in store for us, when for twenty years our tomorrows have brought us nothing but the same tedious repetition? It is in fact the first time that I have gone to bed with some feeling of curiosity, asking myself questions.

December 9

The Authorities are panic stricken: that is what tomorrow held in store for us. One might have foreseen it. First, the abrupt disintegration of the entire electronic network that is one of the motor nerves of the city; then, the death of plastic. What next? And after that? One can easily imagine that the people in power might fear the worst. For instance, the general strike of the laws of electricity. Or the sudden explosion of gas. Or the abrupt disappearance of paper, which would include police records, tax records and bills of indictment, certificates of presence, bills, rent notices, in short the whole pyramid of administration in one wave of nothingness and oblivion.

The government has not taken this risk. And this morning the *Quotidian* announced an unexpected decision of the Center for Distribution of Time: to abandon this gravely compromised month of December so as to create a transitional month between 1999 and 2000, to be called Thircember, the *thir*teenth month in fact, so often mentioned, and never actualized until now.

It will start tomorrow, and none too soon: today, in the heart of winter, the city is in the midst of a heat wave, proving that time and weather are the same. More than 80 degrees in the shade. This is disquieting. If it were to snow this afternoon at such a temperature, one would have reason to doubt everything, even the sky. But nothing could happen more startling than what we've already had: the month of December is over, and yet it is not the new year.

Thircember 1

The month of Thircember is not off to an auspicious start.

The creation of an emergency month was an audacious project of the Center, but the actualization leaves something to be desired.

Since dawn, in fact, a continuous grating noise, obsessive and parasitical, has plunged the entire city in its

presence. The voracious rustling of some millions of lo-
custs, one might think, but it is simply the new time that's
passing, not yet in order, imperfectly decanted.

Unable to make an announcement over the radio or
television, still in blackout, the Center sent out municipal
sound trucks, with people shouting excuses to the citi-
zenry. This disturbs me slightly. If the Center feels the
need to give us excuses, it must be because the situation
is even more critical than it appears.

But I don't care. Late today, I had a bit of news that
effaces all the panic, silences the uproar of the world, ob-
literates all other events: Francine smilingly told me that
the day after tomorrow she will receive the adultery card
that was promised her.

Impossible to sleep tonight. The rustling noise that deaf-
ens us makes less racket in my head than my desire, my
hope, my impatience, my fever. I hear nothing but this:
I am deaf, blind, sealed to all the rest.

Only the day after tomorrow. Let's hope time lasts that
long.

Thircember 2

No one went to work today. No one would have gotten
as far as their office. No way of dealing, in fact, with this
slackening of time, whose effects are felt throughout the
city. To get up, to drag oneself into another room, to dress:
all this takes more than two hours. Every gesture pro-
longs itself in a nightmarish slowness, and any attempt to
change the rhythm, accelerate it, is ridiculously futile. No
one has ever been able to resist time and its laws.

I wanted to profit from this day of respite to write an
official letter of complaint to one of the many Allocations
Treasuries that are all constantly dunning me. I didn't try

it for long. After an hour, I had managed to take a piece of paper, place it before me, and write: "Sirs." Some simple arithmetic, and I saw that by nightfall I would not even have gotten to the point.

I chose, instead, to stay by the window observing the spectacle in the street. It had its charm. The vehicles were advancing no faster than pedestrians, and I had to stare at each passerby to make sure that he was in fact moving, imperceptibly, rather than standing dead in his tracks. Millimeter by millimeter. The most surprising thing I saw was doubtless the accident that took place almost beneath my windows. An ordinary accident, a pedestrian struck by a car. They had been advancing to their collision for half an hour before it occurred. One could have sworn that nothing more serious had happened than a pin striking a feather, but after several minutes I saw that the pedestrian was slowly losing his equilibrium. A quarter of an hour later the pedestrian was stretched out on the street, and the right wheel of the car took about that time to pass over his legs.

If, tomorrow, we were to be beneficiaries of this same time, what an unhoped for joy! Even if making love to Francine would last only a few minutes of normal time, it would then last for several hours. One shadow across the picture: it is quite possible that tomorrow, on the contrary, time will be delivered to us accelerated. That's enough to drive you mad.

Thircember 3

But no, luck is with us.

No temporal disturbances today. Only, these eddies in time have seriously altered certain laws of physics and, although this hardly matters to us, water has changed its density in a matter of seconds. One has had to deploy endless ruses to decant water, to get it out of the faucet. Who cares? We don't plan to make love under water.

"Look," Francine says to me as we leave the subway.

She hands me the adultery card which she has just received. It is not an ordinary card. It is good for three straight days. They didn't string her along: they got her a privileged adultery card, the rarest of all, given out only in absolutely exceptional cases. This gives us time, if time lets us live.

"You're aware, of course," Francine says, "that we have three nights before us."

We reach the hallway of my building. She exhibits her card at the control point, they examine it closely, on principle, punch it, and let us pass. It is nine o'clock. Our first night lies before us. And for the first time we are alone with each other, away from the world with the world's approval.

"It's been a long time," Francine murmurs. "I have the feeling that I have never truly lived except in these few weeks of waiting."

I look at her, I study her liquid gaze, mineral, swampy. I attempt to make out the terror beyond her desire, the astonishment behind the gentleness of her irony, but in vain. It is a look in which it is easier to drown oneself than to read it. The fugitive emotions that pass in her nocturnal pupils are like phantom trains that futilely connect two points impossible to reach. Like me, she is, for the moment, emptied of all save her desire, her thirst. Only the second to live matters to her, the rest can have no reality in her eyes, even if it concerns the fate of the planet, her fate and mine, ours and the others'. We are silent. Now that we are safe from the microphones that no longer can hurt us, far from the private inspectors, the official supervision, the walls with ears, and the floors with eyes, we no longer have anything to say to each other. We have nothing more to fear, to foresee, to think about. We are, therefore we no longer think. We are our only future, our only repast, our only goal, our only essential, our only use of time.

She steps back toward the bed; then, with a few gestures, springs the few clasps of her dress, which falls to the floor in the middle of the room, like a simple peel. She turns slowly around, completely naked, as if to have me admire from all angles the modeling of her body, then falls heavily onto the bed, her hands open, her womb empty, her breasts swollen, her eyes closed. I go to her, I lightly stroke her eyelashes, I caress her neck. I wish I had the ability to discover her slowly, in an imperceptible advance, hair by hair, pore by pore, from vein to vein; but I'm aware that I could never have such patience, any more than she could wait.

"Come," she murmurs, the shadow of a smile on her lips.

I lie down on her, with the feeling of having arrived somewhere, finally.

No question now of waiting or of slow approach, of patience or calculation. There is no time even to press my hand against her belly, when Francine slips away from me as if borne on a violent wave, and it is she who impales herself on me with her full weight, with her whole body and heavy thighs. She falls into love as if hurled into a fourth dimension, convulsive, flayed, burned alive, moaning and taut, maddened and free of everything. She is no more than matter in fusion, a thing wildly alive, an electrode reserve. She no longer sees, hears, or speaks: she is now no more than a prolonged groan, a single gush of pleasure. Contaminated, borne off, gashed, I am lost to myself, possessed by a space which I have never known, rolled aimlessly in a torrent of emptiness in which dozens of mouths suck and pump me with all their warmth.

It was the real thing. Francine belongs to a race of survivors in a world of the living dead: she is simply a human being. A simple feminine female, sexed, exacerbated, tormented, famished, profoundly alive in this vast morgue that is called "our period." Between her and the dummies that surround and beset us, there can be no contact, no reconciliation. She is as out of place in this city, and at this century's end, as a great cat who has been taught to speak and stand on its hind legs.

"I knew," she said to me an hour later.

"I didn't, but I was almost sure of it."

Thircember 4

We fell asleep, glued to each other, towards 6 A.M. And we did not hear the alarm ring. But that no longer mattered. The *Quotidian* announced at one o'clock that no one is allowed to leave his house today. It's incredible, as if we'd bought luck itself. The reason for this peremptory ban, which finds us so happily together, emerged rather clearly for those who got up after having read the paper. "Clearly" one may well say: if the sky seems gray, cloudy, without sun, the light at times has such a brilliance that no one could endure it outside. Evidently, it is to be the day of the unforeseen for which the Center for Distribution of Time bears sole responsibility. But before the authorities had time to send out their orders, between 5 and 7 A.M. thousands of pedestrians had their eyes burnt out. Workers for the most part, so true is it that death often comes to those who rise early, and that work generally leads to the sickbed.

The tone of the article in the *Quotidian* is significant.

It is formal, timorous, humble, and flat. A far cry from the precise, glacial, cutting, authoritarian tone which has always characterized this journal. Something has gone wrong, time is disturbing inexplicably the stablest laws of nature, chemistry's in conflict with physics, mathematics has lost its logic, and the world of elements, calmly unleashed, seems to be readying an assault on the municipal institutions. The authorities seem to fear the worst. They're afraid, you can smell it. They are putting water in their wine, courtesy in their exhortations, smokescreens in their explanations. Their confusion is all the greater in that, for the first time in twenty years, police surveillance and the repressive system have lost their most important weapons: the electronic labyrinth of espionage at all hours, at all levels, despite all obstacles and secret hiding places. Those in authority no longer know precisely what their subordinates are feeling, planning, and saying. They are completely cut off; they may well dread the worst. Not to mention the explosion of imponderables that each day, each day after may bring.

No doubt about it, the Center for Distribution of Time has botched it. This month of Thircember, which one could have taken for an audacious realization of technique, appears above all to be an exemplary failure. One might even ask oneself if, in one way or another, this trial month may not put an end to the flashy exploits of this planet (one cannot imagine what a racket it might have made as a really large planet). In the category of secondary planets, at any rate, it has much to be said for it from the point of view of dementia. Perhaps, it has finally, and after admirable efforts, arrived at another plan: the last.

"You don't think it's the end?" Francine asks, just as I've been thinking this.

"It can't be counted out."

But I have the feeling I'm joking. My only future is limited to the two days that I still have to spend with her, in her, on her, beside her. Afterwards, who cares? Since the law will take her away from me, it may as well take the planet away, too. It would have about the same effect on me as if an old, threadbare rug were removed from under my feet.

Only Francine exists. Francine, and my desire to rend her, my certitude in recording that I truly desired her, that it was no mirage or snare between us, that a night of silence and orgasm justified us, that this young woman was my sole planet of flesh and truth while my native planet has never been anything more for me than a ball of mud, spinach, and concrete.

Objects, with her, take on their true weight, their realest density. When I look at her, when I touch her, everything grows darker, heavier, simpler. A sort of void is created, a penumbra in which there is no more background, nothing superfluous, little nothings, blended details: only an imprecise space in which it's good to lie down, without ever disappearing. There are no more goals to reach, moving objects to contemplate, unbearable noises to endure, situations to unravel. There is nothing but her inertia and her lucidity, which melds with my disdain to create a single night without wreckage, without survivors.

With her, I am total resignation. All's well that ends badly. Or rather not, neither badly nor well. All's well that doesn't begin. I smile, with no reason for smiling, and also no reason for not smiling. I scarcely feel myself. I am neither tired nor in form. I could swear that I have never learnt to read or write, to speak or to reason: that I am no more than a simple empty pod, without brains, muscles, nerves, cells, or arteries. A tube. With an eye at one end, and nothing else. An eye which lucidly sees things, but does not register them, judge them, or transform them into abstractions, thoughts. I am ideally unqualified, indifferent to life, scarcely aware of being alive. I *am* alive of course, but strangely dormant. I am gray, padded, simplified, immunized. Nothing has ever happened, nothing will ever happen again. Only time will pass. In vain, leaving me in place, outside its circuit, far from everything. I have finally realized myself: I was not meant to be much. Now I am what I was meant to be. Before this, I was merely approaching in circles. Now I am at the dead center of this "not much." In the cocoon. Please do not disturb. Useless to disturb: I no longer hear you.

Outside, flashes of blinding light explode, and then what? I merely have to close the shutters, to immure myself here, to close my eyes and draw Francine towards the bed, to find our grave in life there.

"Take me," she murmurs.

Yes. There's really nothing else for me to do. And even if I were asked to replace Christ or give God a hand, I would say: "Terribly sorry. I'm otherwise occupied."

Thircember 5

It's a good question whether the Center for Distribution of Time, with its broken-down experiments, has released, not so much the forces of evil or the wrath of the abstract, but more simply an enormous wave of black humor which nature must have been holding back for us from the beginning of time.

Thus today, while the day commenced in an exceptionally normal manner, suddenly at three o'clock, time stopped. All timepieces halted at exactly the same point for an interval of several seconds. One was bracing oneself for the worst when, just as suddenly, time resumed its flow. Only, and this was rather disquieting, it literally flowed, through all the streets of the city, an enormous yellowish puddle, fortunately quite shallow, and rising at a very slow rate. We've gotten out of it lightly. For the same price, we might have been swept away by a cataract of time and (why not?) a single stream for all of us, in chorus, and our world with us, towards the torrent of the centuries, the profoundest depths of a general flood.

This is, in principle, our last day. The adultery card expires tomorrow morning.

"No," Francine says to me. "I'm staying with you. I will never go back to my place. If they come to arrest me, so what? I still prefer this."

I let her roll herself into a ball, like a cat, to nestle against my stomach. I feel her mouth as she slowly swallows me. I make myself little, too, and hide between her thighs. We are no more than a single cocoon of flesh and softness, fever and refusal to disentangle ourselves. But no one is going to come and arrest or separate us, as I believe now. I don't believe they have the time any more to fuss with us. They must have too many other cases in hand. And cases much more serious, pressing. Strange: only a few days ago, we had the feeling of being spied on, suspected, dogged by all the supervisory agencies of an entire city, while now we have only the feeling of having been forgotten, borne at random in a tranquil and universal catastrophe. We can even abuse the government, spit on our anonymous President-Dictator, join hands in a revolution, shout out our disgust, or yell threats of death: no one will intervene, no one will come to arrest us. There are no more microphones to record our words, no televisions to film our gestures, no more current in the wall plugs, no electricity in the sockets. I even ask myself if there are still policemen or investigators in the streets or offices. Perhaps they are all on their knees, praying for their survival, or extremely busy packing for their trip to the void.

Thircember 6

My hypothesis seems to be borne out.

Panic, and only panic, can explain the decisions of the authorities. Since this morning, a formal ban on reporting to work as well as one on going down into the street at all. The inhabitants are confined to their homes. As a security measure, it's said. But it is clear that the government wishes to avert any possibility of people gathering: they fear crowds, meetings, and groups of workers or employees. They wish to avert any mass action, any attempt to revolt. The State seems to be barking out its last orders, going through its last paces. There's one thing alone which might reassure them: I do believe it's a bit late for starting a revolution. It is the Center for Distribution of Time that holds our future in its hands, a future that seems manifestly compromised. Even the "solution" of taking the Center by storm could not save us. The Center is secretly directed by specialists who are picked and trained by the Ministry of Abstractions, and they are irreplaceable. An act of violence could only plunge the city deeper into an abyss which the Center alone has some chance of retrieving us from. It's too late. We should have thought of revolution earlier. Now, faced with the daily danger of watching time blow up, the political eddies and crosscurrents have but a relative importance. We won't get out of this with slogans, marches, motions, and speeches. Nothing. There is doubtless nothing to do, except wait. That's the sole solution.

And today? Can we credit what happened today to the

Center, which holds the planet between life and death, between the fatal cataclysm and the restorative miracle? It was not much, scarcely an incident, rather harmless and not more unusual than what had preceded, almost re-assuring. In the afternoon, between five and seven, thought was contagious throughout the city, in concentric circles some yards in diameter. It suited me: my only thought was to make love to Francine, and she too, for her part, thought only of this. We will never know which of us contaminated the other. We made love, then, without seeking a response that would have changed nothing between us, anyway.

"And if I had thought of committing suicide?" Francine asks me.

"If you had really thought of it, I would have been contaminated, and we would have committed suicide. I suppose this has happened in many apartments."

Just the same, it was a rather curious experience. Even after making love, I continued to think of nothing else, completely sealed inside this thought, as if buried some inches beneath my own reality. Impossible to get away from it. It evoked rather well those states of mind between dream and slumber when an image, an absurd phrase may recur incessantly, insistently, curiously halting, as if thought slipped as it tried to escape.

Thircember 6(again)

Are things getting worse or not? Hard to say, but they are certainly not getting any clearer. Each day has, inexorably, its unexpected occurrence, and what is down for the day goes by the boards. It proves, more tellingly than ever, the disarray in which the directors of the Center find themselves. Short of solutions, or simply to gain a little time, the Center distributed yesterday for a second time, with a fine unconcern, forcing us all to live it again. I'm not complaining, it was quite agreeable yesterday, and as agreeable this time, but it nonetheless seemed to me a makeshift solution that spoke volumes. No one's stopping the Center from staying right there, seeking no other way out than to leave fifteen million people to tirelessly relive the same incidents, repeat the same gestures until the end of time, to resay the same phrases. I'm for it, I vote yes.

Thircember 7

If the Center is openly displaying its perplexity, it must be recognized that the government is not giving proof of resourceful imagination. I always knew it was more in form, and above all more fit, for arriving at cold-hearted, final, and injurious decisions. At the moment, all it can find to put us off the scent is to offer us phony decisions that can fool no one. Thus, this fine-sounding, empty announcement: In case of emergency, the Central Office of Orders and Prohibitions has transferred its full powers to a Central Office of Prohibitions and Orders. I strongly doubt that this is the moment for juggling with words. But everyone has understood, for some time now, that these changes cannot change anything.

The daily happening proved this, at any rate, better than all the words in the dictionary: announced by a veritable typhoon of municipal fanfare in the morning, the day turned green from nine o'clock on, transforming the entire city into a lugubrious aquarium of the depths. The effect was striking, but terrifying. Nothing could have evoked with more realism the prelude to the end of the world, the dawn of a grand cataclysm.

The panic would no doubt be general were it not dissolved in a sort of stupor which, for the moment, immobilizes the inhabitants. Sometimes I ask myself if the year 2000 will pass us and our planet by. What does it matter? There are so many others.

"I want," says Francine, "to make love with you, but I would like for us to be stuck forever in this instant, softly enfolded, stupefied, almost dead, but not quite."

"We might send in a request to the Center. The shape they're in, they couldn't refuse."

Thircember 8

What happened during the night so far exceeds our most somber expectations that the *Quotidian* has not dared to so much as mention it. But (and this proves that the services of censure and surveillance have completely broken down) the news spread everywhere, by word of mouth. At nine o'clock everyone was discussing it. With terror, and for good reason.

In a single night, after a dangerous distortion of time, all the inhabitants in the northern sector of the city aged ten years. Inexplicably, the phenomenon occurred only in the north; the southern zone in which I reside experienced a normal night. But when does our turn come? In short, if time is not stabilized, and if each night that goes by corresponds to ten years, we have, all of us, including the healthiest, only a few days to live. One must hope that the Center is taking measures without losing an hour, as this virtually means a year.

Thircember 9

Horror has reached its high point, but insanity is gaining on it. Time is having a grand time, and with what a sense of *mise en scène!*

The first page of the *Quotidian* deserves to be framed and bequeathed to future centuries as an example, if one could still believe in future centuries. On page one, in fact, only one miscellaneous item, but endowed with a certain impressive news value: everyone who had the idea of drinking a glass of water this morning at dawn and at 8 A.M. died in a few hours without suffering or apparent cause. It was thought, at first, to be due to a virus, and why not? A temporal virus. That would have been almost normal. But it was not that. The truth was to prove even more singular. All the autopsies revealed an inexplicable and stunning attrition of the cells. The victims swallowed, in fact, not a glass of water, but a glass of time. Free of charge, but what a price! Insane explanation, of course, but exact. It would be corroborated before noon. Suddenly the faucets went dry, but emitted a silky rustling which everyone could recognize: it was what time sounds like when it is poorly filtered, and contains the numerous parasites that the Center sometimes inflicts on us.

Just the same, when time starts flowing through the waterworks, there must be a serious leak somewhere, and a total dereliction of duty on the part of the services concerned. They have utterly lost their grip. From this to clocks giving drinking water as they strike the hour, there is doubtless but a step.

"You're not afraid, are you?" I ask Francine.

"With you, I am not so afraid, no. And you?"

And me? With me, I'm definitely frightened, but with her, slightly less so.

Or perhaps we should still keep hoping? Thousands of sound trucks came racketing through the streets about the precise terms of a major decision which the Center for

Distribution of Time had just taken, at the close of the afternoon: to abandon, as a lost cause, the month of Thircember and to attempt, without delay, starting tomorrow, the junction of the year 1999 and the year 2000.

Thircember 10

It's D Day for Operation 2000.

The Center has officially announced that the transition from 1999 to 2000 is to be effected at four o'clock sharp. There will be a time break of a few seconds only.

There's nothing to do but wait.

10:00

There will be no Christmas Eve this year, with its midnight supper. Too bad, because it would have had its full meaning: who can know, in fact, whether we will get up tomorrow morning?

Noon

Contrary to all expectations, since this morning, everything seemed to be for the best in the best of all possible centuries. Not only was time flowing normally, but it made almost no rustling noise, and water also poured from the faucets, very clear and nontoxic. We were able to look forward to the future, and the temporal soldering which the Center would attempt in fours hours. Or, on the contrary, feel some degree of panic at the idea that we could, despite everything, *have* a future.

Until the moment when, at about ten in the morning, things oxidized.

This began with an incident which had not yet figured

in the catalogue of home disasters, recently recorded: suddenly, sounds did not resonate in space, as if swallowed by the void. Then, almost immediately, the echoes were restored; but, as if the air were simply a reservoir of short circuits, each sound provoked its own luminous static, creating over the entire city a single fireworks display composed of millions of ephemeral little squibs, immediately replaced by others. Then, for several seconds, all metal objects became as malleable as fresh butter, while everything red inexplicably turned green. This interlude was followed without transition by an episode which everyone had dreamt about: all the pigeons in the city died simultaneously, victims of a mysterious scourge that left them no time to suffer. It was then, at almost the same instant, that all the windows in the city shattered, just as everything in glass exploded in splinters, although nothing obstensibly had happened to cause this. The power failure, which lasted only two minutes, seemed normal, and made no one nervous, but the glacial wind that sprung up with it was a sign of nothing good. It fell, however, when the lights came back. There ensued a lull which was abruptly broken by a solemn burst of thunder, rending a blue sky that contained not one cloud.

Then, silence.

As if God had spoken or farted for the last time.

At noon sharp, in fact, as if these events were happening on schedule, equilibrium was restored. The sky, the weather, the air, the mild breeze, the temperature, objects, atmospheric pressure, echoes, everything.

1 P.M.

Everything is calm.

The whole city is holding its breath. Outside, there is

not a single vehicle, almost no pedestrians, and no traffic at all. One could hear a fly buzzing around this gigantic cement basin, which has always been known as a reservoir of noise.

For the moment, nothing is happening; but from one minute to the next, one expects the worst. People have realized that anything can happen. And what, exactly, is in store for us? A reverse of time? A flood of time via the waterworks? An avalanche of anachronisms? A cyclone of simultaneities? An isochronic storm of continuity? An explosion of chronologies? A collision of concordances of time? What is going to happen to us? Are we about to record the disappearance of one of the three dimensions? Or perhaps colors are going to vanish into the waterworks, only to flow through the faucets into our sinks? Unless we suppose that we will find ourselves abruptly thrown back into a past century, that is well before our birth, and then into one well after our death? Or into an anterior or conditional future in which, also, we cannot survive? Or more simply, following time through the pipes, we will be obliged to turn into larvae, and adapt ourselves as well as we can to our new submarine and subterranean existence? Or perhaps time, from having been masticated and put through futile tests, will break into two portions, and we will live simultaneously on two planes, in 1999 and 2000? Just as we may be about to see the whole city subside into dead time, and vanish, lock, stock, and barrel. Or will all lost time suddenly surge up from its secret nothingness, to raze everything in a single, terrifying current of hours, more deadly than a cyclone? Or, like a waterspout collapsing, will all the dust of time bury this civilization and its promoters, in less time than it takes to say it?

Gratuitous, far-fetched hypotheses? Not any more than others, not any less than the avalanche of the unforeseen we've been subjected to for fifteen days.

2:00

Time has not flowed as normally as this in a very long time. The clocks, at two, struck twice, and twice only. It's incredible. Time is actually passing. Well regulated, well filtered, and silent. Has the Center succeeded in impaling the imponderables, wringing their necks like that of a vulgar little hen? Has it redressed the situation heading for disaster? One might actually think so.

It's more than a question of thinking, now. It's much more a question of simply getting through the time, to achieve it, to float on this ocean of centuries which is one great gulf in which the planet risks foundering. Just revenge for things: man has never been more than a thinking reed, and now has suddenly been reduced to a floating reed.

2:30

Francine is coiled on the bed, almost rolled into a ball, singularly folded in on herself, sealed in herself, very calm, silent and unmoving. She rests her chin on her elbow, and seems to look at me less than to breathe me in to the depths of her clear somber gaze, transliquid, swampy-carnivorous, the disquieting gaze of an adult child who expresses more easily the unfathomable than the usual exact feelings.

"You look like a cat," I tell her.

She's slightly surprised.

"A cat? That was an animal, wasn't it?"

"That's right, you've never known one. It was an enchanting animal. They did away with them a long time ago, because they evoked idleness."

"Did you like them?"

"When I was a child, I always used to sleep with one."

She smiles, relaxed, submissive, but there is something so morbid, tenderly morbid in her smile, that it frightens me a little. It's true that she seems in complete accord with the end of all things, a mild expectation at the threshold of the void, as available as the last hour of life, harmful and alluring as a velvet snare of night, of quietness and warm enfolding.

"Come to me, lie down on me," she says with a peculiar, fixed smile.

I come. Before flowing into her, I wind up my alarm clock, and set it for this evening. If I should fall asleep, I want, at least, to wake up at four, so as not to miss our entry into another century. Let's hope it's not our entry into another world . . .

3:00

The seconds record themselves with an admirable minuteness, admirably seconded by the hours which pass regularly, one after the other, making one believe that the Center is having an easy time with time.

All hopes are permissible.

In one hour, watch in hand, we will begin the history of a new century. As for the planet, its environment, its inhabitants and animals, one may hope that it will not resemble that of the previous century. I doubt strongly whether this world could survive, for another century, such a deluge of delirium and horror, of insanity and aberrations, of nightmares and ugliness.

And what if this hour were the world's last? I take this hypothesis to be as plausible as any other: I try to envisage it; I confront it and I feel nothing in particular. No panic, no anguish or revolt. I feel less frightened, in fact, than on certain days when things were going neither well nor badly, less terrorized than I was on the tennis courts, under the vacation sun, bathed in the pale illumination of work, or in the deceivingly mild twilight of certain evenings. Francine has caused me to lose a sense of reality; she has effaced everything that is not her skin, her belly, her thighs, her cries, her silence, her breathing, or her climate. I turn towards her, I teeter towards her, I lose equilibrium, memory, feeling, everything except my need for her. I forget everything, therefore I am.

I have time, even if the world has only an hour to live.

An hour is evidently not much time in which to reconstruct the pyramids, invent a new detergent, fuse trigonometry and applied morality, destroy the reconstructed pyramids, resolve *in extremis* the disquieting problem of the duettists Kisomnou and Houallongnou, descend to the depths of the sea, and afterward scale the highest earthly peak, repyramid the pyramids, sharpen twelve thousand pencils by hand, establish the groundwork for the tenth art, pyramid once more the pyramids, break the record for swimming across the Atlantic, earn enough to pay off one's contributions before the last minute, and finally perch on the summit of the pyramids to contemplate, from the top of this pile of stones, the twenty-four centuries as they crumble. It's not much, an hour, to do all this, no it isn't. You can't even get two office hours out of an hour. But it is enough time in which to make love to Francine. For me alone, an hour is a lot.

"You don't happen to have the time, do you?"

"I'm sorry, sir, but it may be the last, and it is taken."

3:50

"In ten minutes, we enter the year 2000!" yell the sound

trucks which the Center has sent out through the city.

Deprived of microphones and loudspeakers, the voices echo shrilly through megaphones. It's really rather pathetic. It sounds likes the narrator's voice, clogged with phlegm and fake enthusiasm, announcing some third-rate film in a provincial cinema. The government has not only lost face, and its electronic toys, and its police, and its power to strike; it has also lost its arrogance and its pretension. This is not far from having the event of the century announced to us by a rural constable preceded by a drummer.

3:55

It is still early; it is already late. I am tired; I feel tired, and Francine seems even more tired than I. At least if she had the energy to turn to me, to answer to her name when I called her, and to breathe against my neck a word which no one will ever hear. I could almost swear that she is dying, that she has spurted into my veins her last spasm of life. I get up, I hold her face between my two hands and turn it toward me: I have the sensation of moving about at the bottom of an abyssal trough. I speak, and I could swear that my words can no longer travel through air. But she hears me, even if her expression is that of a somnambulistic stranger, who has never heard anyone.

"Do you think you'll go home, in the twenty-first century?" I ask her.

"My home is here."

"Will you leave it?"

"No. I will not go back. I won't budge from here. I love you."

"I love you, too."

4:00

"Attention!" the voice resumes. "We are about to pass from the year 1999 to the year 2000. In exactly fifteen seconds, the Center will make an incision in time of a few minutes, during which we will quit the twentieth century for the dawn of the twenty-first century. Attention! Five . . . four . . . three . . . two . . . one. ZERO and now . . ."

"And now . . ."

Then, nothing more.

With this last word, this agonized hiccup, the world entered forever into silence. At the end, as in the beginning, there was the word.

The planet never made it into the twenty-first century. Time, in fact, had not been put to rights, and man never recovered from it.

VERY
SINCERELY
YOURS

THE ADVENTURE STORY BOOK CLUB/Paris

Paris, August 11, 1955

Monsieur Strigel
Xeriac-sur-Alphe

Dear M. Strigel,

No, sir, you do not know me.

Neither do I know you, it must be said. Nevertheless, I am writing to you. It is even, to be quite exact, the fourth time that I've written to you, since you have already sent us three complaints previously about the book which you have not received, and each time I've had to answer you. What do you expect? We have our principles in such matters—slightly ridiculous, but very strict: every letter merits a response, it seems. And we observe this motto, of course, *to the letter,* in all its noble antiquity.

I am, then, answering you for the fourth time. But this time I will not talk to you about the book which you have not yet received. We will, if it's all right with you, dispense with this gloomy, painful subject. Besides, I don't see how I could talk to you about it, since I threw your letter into the wastepaper basket without reading it. It was at that very instant, I believe, that I decided to write to you. To really write to you.

Why?

Because I don't know you. That is the first reason, the most important no doubt.

Because in my eyes, you represent not so much the Unknown as the Void, Nothingness, total Anonymity. I am therefore able to talk to you without emotion, without purpose or theme, without the slightest trace of feeling. It's a little as if I'd suddenly decided to write to a wall. A living wall, if you like. For I know that my letter will arrive at a destination, and that there will be a face to read it there, hands to throw it away.

That is why this morning I have written to you. And I will write to you every day. Regularly.

Very sincerely yours,

J.S., DIRECTOR

THE ADVENTURE STORY BOOK CLUB/Paris

Paris, 8/12/55

Monsieur Strigel
Xeriac-sur-Alphe

Dear M. Strigel,

First of all, I must clarify a point which may be of importance. All my letters are signed "J.S., Director." But it is obvious that I am not J.S., the Director. If I were, I would not be here, and I would not be writing to you. My proof? It is that Monsieur J.S. is not here, that he has never written to you, and doubtless never will. He has other ways of amusing himself, and can one really blame him?

No need explaining that I am not officially representing Monsieur J.S., the Director, either. I do not have his powers, his signature, or even his privileges. And what, exactly, do I represent, then? I represent his typewriter. I am the typewriter of J.S., the Director. I don't think, I write. Automatically, of course. On the one hand, all letters resemble each other, all use the same watered-down language to express the same complaints, the same satisfaction. On the other hand, dexterity is the daughter of habit, and I, for my part, have long since reached this stage. This does not tell you who I am, but we shall certainly have occasion to broach this subject. Not a very exciting one, I'm afraid.

Of course, you could write personally to Monsieur J.S., the Director, informing him that the employee in charge of correspondence has had the audacity to send you, for two days running already, letters which are far removed from any conceivable business purpose, and which seem near insane. You could, yes. But how is it that I know you won't? You will not bring this matter to the Director's attention. Why? I don't know. But that's the way it is. This letter, then, will be the second in a long series.

Very sincerely yours,

J.S., DIRECTOR

P.S. Since I don't have the good fortune to be called J.S., my name is Claude Gardère.

THE ADVENTURE STORY BOOK CLUB/Paris

Paris, August 14, 1955

Monsieur Strigel
Xeriac-sur-Alphe

Dear M. Strigel,

Refusal . . .

Doubtless you've already guessed it . . . it is what has always lain between my future and myself like a wall or moat. The refusal to simply accept what others will, most often with the feeling of a duty accomplished. How do they do it? I myself have never been able to.

Nevertheless, one must live. At least, one has said so so often that one ends up believing it. And so I accept, generally for a few months. Then lucidity intervenes. Then boredom gives way to agony, dread to absolute inertia. As if a safety valve had suddenly opened inside me, and flooded me with a sort of drunkenness, translated into an irreducible desire to flee.

Just words, you believe? But these words sum up ten years of my life. For it is ten years, M. Strigel, that I have been working, and I have achieved nothing. I haven't advanced an inch. There isn't one situation I've gotten the better of. I haven't even managed to save a cent—for what, anyway?—it's been ten years since I began my business career with a company for the minimum living wage provided by law. I have just been hired by another firm for the same minimum wage. Between these two identical poles, I have run through twenty jobs or so. I have left all of them of my own free will. But my desire to quit is still with me. To say "no" for no particular reason, a proclamation of faith no doubt.

I cannot even say that I am a victim of bad luck. On the contrary, I have always been hired by understanding bosses, by real human beings on occasion. Some of them went so far as to understand me; others attempted to reason with me. I was a "case" for them. They enjoyed understanding that they didn't understand me. There were even those who made every possible allowance for me, to give me my chance. What they believed to be a "chance": a job, responsibilities, directives, and genuinely professional feelings. I don't have to tell you that this kind of "chance" meant absolutely nothing to me.

Well, for the moment, that's all I have to say to you.

Very sincerely yours,

J.S., DIRECTOR

THE ADVENTURE STORY BOOK CLUB/Paris

Paris, 8/16/55

Monsieur Strigel
Xeriac-sur-Alphe

Dear M. Strigel,

Already several days have passed since I sent my first letter to your address. This delay reassures me. Nothing, in fact, has happened: you have not sent an indignant letter to the Directorship. You have not lodged a complaint with the mental health authorities. You have not even sent me a threatening letter, telling me to stop writing immediately, or else . . .

In fact, you have not responded. You accept. And to deduce from this that you approve is hardly unreasonable. At any rate, I believe I can say that you have understood my secret hope: to write to silence. You have observed the rules of the game, and now we may continue it.

Today, I am writing you at the end of the day. I have

to tell you that there was a very considerable lag in my correspondence. Each day has added to this lag, and each new batch of mail has robbed me of the courage I need to set about this task. A moment came when I was even afraid to take up or open the portfolio which contained this correspondence. Then, this morning, I opened it, and set to work. I got through it rather easily. But then, I have certain talents, as I've already told you. What's missing above all is the talent to use these talents. An incurable malady. You know, as I do, of course, that delinquents and crazy people are locked up, that the seriously ill are sent to hospitals or sanatoriums, but for the incurable misfits, the passive by nature, nothing has been provided. For years I have been searching for a doctor who could understand my case, and be willing to write out a lifetime work exemption for me, on grounds of "mental incapacity." It seems to me that the anguish of living is a disease as serious as any. But doctors, like directors of companies, are realistic men. They would find a way to make full-time employment, at 100 percent profit, for a cripple, a person who was dying, or even someone who was not yet born.

I have, like anyone else, responsibilities and burdens to assume. A pretty formula, in fact. I have acquired a certain amount of personal property, and I am the owner in perpetuity. I have rented my life for a number of years: an apartment, a wife, then a child, water and gas, a cat, electricity. All this is very decorative, it furnishes time and space, but it is rather expensive. Sometimes I think of escape. To get up one morning as usual, head for the office, and suddenly, halfway there, stop. To refuse to go farther. And then turn tail and run away. But a few minutes of meditation are enough to convince me that flight is impossible. Instead of going farther, I would be going elsewhere. This means exactly the same thing, in reality. I would be abandoning certain leases, only to immediately accept others. Instead of renting a job, an apartment, and a wife, I would be renting a train, other women, and other jobs. Everything always ends in a job, that's obvious. It's even a job to do nothing. And not an easy one, either. Even if one accepts exactly what's on hand and waiting, and is inclined to refuse everything else, how does one annul the lease which we have signed simply by being alive? That is the heart of the problem, the heart of the abyss as well: the fact that between life and death there is no intermediate solution. We must either live or die. This fantastic paucity of choice has always filled me with consternation.

That is why, today, I have caught up on my correspondence. That is why, tomorrow, I will continue this task.

Very sincerely yours,

J.S., DIRECTOR

THE ADVENTURE STORY BOOK CLUB/Paris
Paris, 8/18/55

Monsieur Strigel
Xeriac-sur-Alphe

Dear Sir,

When one thinks about it—and I am thinking about it for the first time since writing to you—it's a rather curious name, Strigel. It sounds somewhat German, but that no doubt is a mistake. Strigel—one has the impression that it is a common name, that one has already heard it, but then, on reflection, one realizes that nobody has this name. But can a name be important? Whether you're called Rigel, Igel, or Strigel, it changes nothing. Anyway, this is the first time that I have really thought about you. Why, I ask myself.

Aside from this, I have handed in my resignation to the office. By mail, last night. It was a sudden decision. Maybe it was because the boredom of writing commercial letters to unknown destinations acquired such density yesterday that I suddenly felt the need to write a *noncommercial* letter with a very *precise* destination. Since I could not give as an explanation for my quitting the fact that the boredom had truly exceeded my capacities, I stated in the letter that the correspondence had given me epistolary flu, an illness of which little is known, but which may be contagious, therefore dangerous in a place as public as a business office. I saw the director this morning. He had my letter in his hand, and kept shaking his head as he stared at me.

"You will never change, I suppose," he said.

No, doubtless not. But I will change jobs and places. To no end, I know. All roads lead to the office, and all office exits open on office entrances. The city, of course, is nothing but a gigantic cash register in which there are millions of little compartments, or offices. I will find everywhere the same faces, the same calendars, the same walls larded with files and portfolios. Perhaps even the same brand of typewriter. And the same boredom, as you can guess.

I have, then, no more than forty-two letters left to write to you. Perhaps less. Certainly not more. Strange, I regret it slightly.

Very sincerely yours,

J.S., DIRECTOR

Xeriac-sur-Alphe, 8/19/55

Monsieur Gardère
The Adventure Story Book Club
Paris

Dear Sir,

    A pity.
    Your letters interested me.
    I have the pleasure, sir, of being your humble servant.

                            S. STRIGEL

THE ADVENTURE STORY BOOK CLUB/Paris
Paris, 8/20/55

Monsieur Strigel
Xeriac-sur-Alphe

Dear Sir,

    You aren't a wall, then. You answered my last letter. Did I feel any surprise? I don't think so. On the one hand, it has been a long time since I could experience any precise feeling. On the other, I believe I knew that one day you would respond to my letters. I note, however, with some pleasure that it no longer concerns a book you haven't gotten, or your complaints about our organization. Short as your letter is, it is addressed in confidence to me personally. It is the first such letter I have had. And I am happy to see that you have dismissed from your mind the Club and its moronic activities. You'll profit from the switch, believe me, if from nothing else. The book, for us, is as anonymous as a tin of preserves, and hardly worth your second thought. You're better off without it. Man's most negative, detestable contrivance is the product for sale.

But where do I get this strange certainty that your letter is only the first of a series of other letters? And that these letters have a concealed purpose? Something sensational, even. But this intuition of mine is ridiculous. How could your letters cause any repercussion in my life? Thunder out of heaven couldn't change it. I'm used to tempests. One comes out of them drenched, but the night passes, and by the next day, at dawn, one has dried off.

Very sincerely yours,

J.S., DIRECTOR

Xeriac-sur-Alphe

Monsieur Gardère
The Adventure Story Book Club
Paris

Dear Sir,

It should be said that "thunder out of heaven" is not much to be afraid of. In no way could this pass for a sensational event, even a secondary one. But there are others.

Yes, there may be a purpose behind my letters.

May I tell you something which has struck me in your letters? You really lack curiosity. There is not a trace of it in you. A rather commonplace fact, of course, but it may have its importance.

Very sincerely yours,

S. STRIGEL

THE ADVENTURE STORY BOOK CLUB/Paris

Paris, 8/22/55

Monsieur Strigel
Xeriac-sur-Alphe

Dear Sir,

It's true, I'm not curious, I distrust curiosity. We know where it drags us, rather than where it leads us. In general, it ends in something like the passion for stamp collecting, greed, or useless rummaging through bureau drawers.

Nevertheless, one detail does intrigue me. I've been thinking about it since I noticed it. You live in Xeriac-sur-Alphe. And this is an actual fact, since my letters have reached you at that address: you've answered them. And yet your letters are postmarked "Paris." Not being curious, I only noticed it this morning. But notice it I did. Today, I think about it and I ask myself certain questions. Why do your letters carry a Paris postmark? Is it because Xeriac-sur-Alphe is merely a suburb of Paris, so that every morning, when you go into the city, you mail your letters from the 8th arrondissement? But why have I never heard of a neighborhood with this name?

And, suddenly, this name, which before seemed so banal to me, seems to acquire a strange resonance. What *departement* is Xeriac-sur-Alphe located in? Shall I make you a confession? We at the Club are known for our painstaking thoroughness. We possess a dictionary of the administrative districts of France. A complete one, of course. I looked in it in vain for Xeriac-sur-Alphe. First I looked under Xeriac. Then Alphe. I was even naive enough to doublecheck. Do I have to tell you what you know al-

ready? Nowhere did I find Xeriac-sur-Alphe.
May I ask you where Xeriac-sur-Alphe is?

> Very sincerely yours,
>
> J.S., DIRECTOR

Xeriac-sur-Alphe, 8/23/55

Monsieur Gardère
The Adventure Story Book Club
Paris

Dear Sir,

I am genuinely surprised.

Are you sure you really looked for it? Is your edition of
the dictionary the most recent? "Xeriac" is written with an
"X" as in Xenophon and xenophobia. I have the very same
dictionary before me, and I read, plain as day, "Xeriac-sur-
Alphe, population 4,567,000, capital of Alastraze." It seems
to me that there is some misunderstanding. Perhaps we
are not talking of the same dictionary of administrative
districts?

I leave you to your research. But I look forward to
receiving an early confirmation from you.

> With best wishes,
>
> S. STRIGEL

THE ADVENTURE STORY BOOK CLUB/Paris
Paris, 8/24/55

Monsieur Strigel
Xeriac-sur-Alphe

Dear Sir,

I might have sent you a reproachful or threatening letter. I might also have said that this had gone far enough, that you are teasing me. Or else I might have said that my sense of humor has had enough exercise, and is giving up.

I will say none of these things.

Why? Because I believe you. Exactly: I take your assertions literally. I know that they are true. Unlikely, of course, but true. You are not lying, and you're not making fun of me. You really do live in Xeriac-sur-Alphe, a city of 4,567,000 inhabitants, the capital of Alastraze. No point in telling you that there is no capital by this name on the face of the earth. What must be deduced from this? That you do not live on Earth. That is exactly what I *have* deduced.

May I offer you my congratulations? You have the good luck not to live on Earth, and whatever your lot may be "elsewhere," I believe in it more than in mine. I envy you, dear sir, and I tell you so in all frankness.

I believe I can understand, now, why your letters gave me a tacit impression of something exciting. But what? One fact still seems rather strange to me: how have your letters reached me when the name "Xeriac-sur-Alphe" can only be a mystery or joke for any postal clerk in the world? And how can you reply to me by return post?

All this might be quite exciting. But this adventure, you see, like any other, is not enough for me. It doesn't exalt me; it in no way changes the boredom which I assume with all my professional responsibility. It is unusual, to be sure, slightly weird, unforeseen. But it's to no end. It doesn't even seem very surprising to me, when I think it over.

Could you nonetheless answer my question?

Thank you, and my sincerest compliments.

J.S., DIRECTOR

Xeriac-sur-Alphe

Monsieur Gardère
The Adventure Story Book Club
Paris

Dear Sir,

Is it possible that, despite your indifference for your surroundings, you are a logical soul craving for explanations? In that case, my reply will disappoint you. To explain how I, the inhabitant of another world, receive your letters, and how you receive mine, is impossible. For several reasons. First of all, because I am not a technician: this question involves a complex agency of which I know almost nothing. Next, because if I gave you precise explanations, you would be incapable of understanding them. The whole structure is in fact based on a logic which is foreign to you, and which is, I assure you, very far removed from the principles of your mathematics or your geometry as such. Besides, if I were to unveil to you certain workings of our civilization, you would take me for a madman. Or else, and this is more probable, you would not believe me.

Better, then, to stick to hypotheses.

At any rate, you have one fact as proof: there is no city on Earth called Xeriac-sur-Alphe, and yet you have been corresponding for some weeks now with an inhabitant of that city. Isn't that enough for you? And I can tell you that you are not the only one to correspond with Xeriac-sur-Alphe. Other Earthlings have done likewise, most of them without knowing it.

What can you expect? We like letters. But it is not simply to indulge our epistolary passion that we are doing this. Nor is it for purposes of information, either. We have known enough about you for some time. Of course, certain concepts escape us. Such as the circle, fire, division, and others. But what need have we for these concepts, since our world is based on others which escape you?

But rest assured. . . . There will be time for revelations. And perhaps you will understand, one day, why I am writing to you.

Very sincerely yours,

S. STRIGEL

THE ADVENTURE STORY BOOK CLUB/Paris
Paris, 8/26/55

Monsieur Strigel
Xeriac-sur-Alphe

Dear Sir,

Your world, you say, is ignorant of certain concepts such as the circle, fire, and division. I am not so surprised. Is it equally ignorant of boredom? For *our* world, I must tell you, is much more subject to boredom than to the laws of spatial geometry. This morning, for instance, dear sir, the boredom seemed to me to be of such density that I am sapped of the capacity for surprise. Believe me: how happy I would be if I could interest myself in your revelations, make them a subject for meditation against the coming day! Alas! I haven't managed to. Boredom is my sole subject for meditation. This in no way detracts from the potential for the unforeseen, and even the extraordinary, that your letters contain. But then again, what can possibly change my life?

I, too, am not a technician. When I asked you how it was that we were able to correspond, it was not so much curiosity that inspired my question as indifference, no doubt. Just as every morning one asks one's neighbor, "How are you?" Besides, even if you had been able to give me logical explanations, I would not have understood them. Nothing is stranger for me than an abstract explanation. This leads me to make you a confession: I am not a very intelligent man. Perhaps you have made an unfortunate choice in writing to me. But then, perhaps you are not very intelligent either? Who knows? Perhaps, tens of millions of miles away, you perform the same humiliating, ridiculous function as myself? Perhaps you are nothing more than a modest office worker who is distracting himself by sending messages out into the void? I can't help but approve. You have found an excellent distraction. Rather unexpected, in fact. As for whether it does you any more good than playing pool . . .

Very sincerely yours,

J.S., DIRECTOR

Xeriac-sur-Alphe

Monsieur Gardère
The Adventure Story Book Club
Paris

Dear Sir,

No, I am not an office worker. What I am about to tell you will doubtless make you wonder: we have not yet invented the Office. But this will come, perhaps. Or perhaps we imagined it so many centuries ago that we have forgotten it.

You believe that this letter, like the others, has been typed. You believe this because, on Earth, it is usual to employ a typewriter in order to type letters. In our world, things happen differently. This letter has not been written. And yet it exists. It has not been "prepared." But it has its reality. It is not a mirage. How were we able to do this? This, like the rest, would take us too far. And, as you have specified, technical games do not interest you.

All of this notwithstanding, I do have what you would call a function. That of corresponding with Earth. It is not by chance, then, that I correspond with your firm. Not by chance, nor as a game, nor for distraction.

You also mention "intelligence." I find it very awkward to answer you on this score. Among us, it is never a question of intelligence. This notion also is unknown to us. We have read your numerous treatises on this subject. We have never understood them. But as you see, we are doing fairly well without it.

Very sincerely yours,

S. Strigel

THE ADVENTURE STORY BOOK CLUB/Paris
Paris, 8/28/55

Monsieur Strigel
Xeriac-sur-Alphe

Dear Sir,

What you have said does in fact make me wonder. In my most demented dreams of other worlds, I have never been able to imagine one without offices. This, more than anything else, proves that your world is really rather astonishing. This truly does pass the limits of the inconceivable. Whether you are two-dimensional larvae living in cells, or enormous stems that live only for an hour, or multiform yet solid odors, I will easily accept it. But a civilized world without *offices* . . . I almost suspect you of lying . . .

But what in fact are you, Monsieur Strigel? How are you? Biped, mammiferous like myself, with these two eyes full of nothing, this perfect nose, this sensual mouth, and this willful chin which has always been the greatness and the fame of man? Or are you oviparous, lactaceous, acromicephalous, invertebrate? Or what?

Of course, I cannot compel a member of the Club to reveal something to me unless he sees fit to. For, whatever may happen, you are still a member of our Club. This reminds me that, for the others, you are merely a file number lost among thousands of other numbers. It also reminds me that, for some time now, you have not ordered any of our books. What's the matter? Have our works disappointed you? If you have some complaint you would like to address to us, please do not hesitate. We are here to satisfy your needs, and your pleasure is our sole concern.

Very sincerely yours,

J.S., DIRECTOR

Xeriac-sur-Alphe, 8/29/55

Monsieur Gardère
The Adventure Story Book Club
Paris

Dear Sir,

I have no complaints concerning the Club. I happen to know about the subjects which you are dealing with now, and they do not interest me. I should say that we have good reason for knowing the history of Earth much better than you know it. During the Middle Ages, in fact, we landed on Earth rather frequently. But since the eighteenth century, we've fallen out of the habit of visiting your world. It has lost all interest for our navigators. We prefer other worlds, more distant and more salubrious. And then, you are always talking, always on the move. And aggressive as well, it must be added.

What am I like? Why, it's more than likely, dear sir, that I resemble you like a brother. With two eyes, of course, a brow, a mouth, and chin. And two arms and legs. Five fingers. Like you, biped.

At the very most, I am older than you. I was born in 1254. I have reached what is called the prime of life. But this is a mere detail. It in no way modifies my appearance.

One question for now. How many people have subscribed to your Club? I don't refer to the publicity figure. I mean the real number.

Very sincerely yours,

S. STRIGEL

THE ADVENTURE STORY BOOK CLUB/Paris
Paris, 8/30/55

Monsieur Strigel
Xeriac-sur-Alphe

Dear Sir,

I should feel some scruple in answering your last question. You ask how many members we have at present in our Club. And you want the real number. This is a request which is contrary to all our commercial principles. Upon reflection, I am nonetheless going to answer you. I only hope that you will not utilize my response for commerical ends. But in fact, what trouble could it make for me? The whole question would be to know if the founding of another Club in another galaxy could affect our sales, and appear to be dangerous competition for us. Frankly, I don't think so.

We have asserted, for the past few months, that the Club has a membership of 54,650, but in reality we have only 21,564. Generally speaking, one should divide all propaganda figures by two.

I hope that this answer will satisfy you, and that it will be of some use.

Very sincerely yours,

J.S., DIRECTOR

Xeriac-sur-Alphe, 8/31/55

Monsieur Gardère
The Adventure Story Book Club
Paris

Dear Sir,

Your response is in fact useful in a certain way for me. May I tell you that I am slightly disappointed? I thought there were more members in your Club. Twenty-one thousand is not very many.

Allow me, nonetheless, to reveal to you why I have requested this information. In the very near future, we intend to launch a little advertising campaign on Earth. That is to say, we plan to make ourselves known. Not by landing on your planet, but by correspondence. By a series of fliers which will provide precious information on our customs, our world, our civilization, and our way of life. This may be taken as a joke, but we are determined to give it a try.

We have been thinking about it for a long time. Now, I am not in contact merely with you and your Club. I am in touch with most of the events on Earth, by correspondence. And, very soon, I shall have to ask a little favor from certain of my correspondents. I believe that some of them will decline, but I am sure that you, at least, will not refuse me. But perhaps I am wrong.

Very sincerely yours,

S. STRIGEL

THE ADVENTURE STORY BOOK CLUB/Paris
Paris, 9/1/55

Monsieur Strigel
Xeriac-sur-Alphe

Dear Sir,

This service which you are counting on me for, I will of course do for you. I speak of it with a certain assurance because I believe I know what it's about.

Rest assured that it will be very easy for me to do it. I am personally responsible for the mailing of circulars to the 21,000 members of the Club, and to slip your fliers in with our circulars will be very easy for me. All that is necessary is that I have the documents in time. No one will be told about it, and everything will go off nicely.

Can you send me, at once, a copy of this flier? And do you plan to send it throughout the whole world at the same time? This, to me, would seem the most effective technique. But I leave it to you alone to decide. As a publicist, I have always been told that only the bulk mailing works. This, of course, is only a terrestrial law . . .

Very sincerely yours,

J.S., DIRECTOR

Xeriac-sur-Alphe, 9/2/55

Monsieur Gardère
The Adventure Story Book Club
Paris

Dear Sir,

It is a true pleasure to work with you. I thank you for grasping the situation so clearly. Doubtless you have guessed that I have little time to spare, and that, by nature, I am not loquacious. You have spared me many useless explanations.

We are ignorant of the essential laws of publicity, but we also believe that it would be more efficient to send out all our fliers at the same time. Alas! As we are in contact with 6,784 firms on Earth, it will not be possible to orchestrate the operation in this fashion. But we trust that all our fliers will be in the mails by October 1st.

By the same post, I am sending you the 22,000 fliers that you will need. I enclose a copy of this flier. As you will see for yourself, it is not very elegant. It is a simple folder. Yours, of course, is written in French. This flier has been printed in fifty-seven languages.

What it says is clear enough. It states that, many light years away from you, there is a planet called Agonese the Luminous, and that civilized beings live there, die there, think there. There follow explanations of the topography of our planet, its evolution, its climate, and precious information on the civilization which we have created there. As I have already told you, this tourist flier may be taken for a joke. But we have inserted a postscript with a few practical exercises in physics, chemistry, and mathematics which, absurd in the eyes of the ignorant, will certainly cause your intellectuals and specialists in figures to take us seriously. They will certainly not think it is a joke. No man on your Earth could think up such a joke. These exercises contain enough imponderable factors to give rise to the liveliest doubt, and stupefaction. I promise you a real revolution will occur in a very short while. Do you understand? I spoke to you of a goal and an event concealed behind my letters. I was not wrong.

With my full thanks for the service which you are about to render me, I beg you to believe, Sir, in my most distinguished sentiments.

S. STRIGEL

THE ADVENTURE STORY BOOK CLUB/Paris
Paris, 9/3/55

Monsieur Strigel
Xeriac-sur-Alphe

Dear Sir,

Shall I make a confession? The arrival of your flier has all but roused me from the torpor which is my natural state. I must say, this folder is exciting reading, and does contain a surefire potential for novelty. I understood none of the scientific exercises, but they seemed to me sufficiently baffling. There is, in all this, a tone which, from all the evidence, is not of Earth. Not even of the confused and secret world of insanity. I begin to believe that you are right. This deluge of circulars may well cause a sensation.

It will happen soon enough, I think.

We shall have the first repercussions a few days from now, since the 22,000 fliers which you entrusted to me were all sent out yesterday evening. With the circular announcing the publication of *The Inca Adventure* by M. Bertrand Flornoy. A rather scathing irony. . . . How laughable *The Inca Adventure* appears when one thinks of the Adventure contained in the flier from your world. I hope that the contrast will escape no one. But you can't rely on people: they are lacking in imagination, or else their sense of the "serious" is so fantastically developed . . .

Very sincerely yours,

J.S., DIRECTOR

Xeriac-sur-Alphe, 9/4/55

Monsieur Gardère
The Adventure Story Book Club
Paris

Dear Sir,

You have my full gratitude. Your acting so quickly has deeply moved me.

You have, then, mailed out the first batch of our fliers throughout your world. But this despatch will soon be followed by a number of others. As of now, in fact, I figure on 356 mailings throughout various countries, and estimate that in a few days some twenty million people will have received the fliers from our world. From then on, certainly, there will be repercussions.

I will have much to do, and no doubt will not write to you for several days. I ask you not to take this as a sign of indifference on my part, but simply as an indication that I cannot do so.

With my most cordial sentiments.

S. STRIGEL

THE ADVENTURE STORY BOOK CLUB/Paris
Paris, 9/5/55

Monsieur Strigel
Xeriac-sur-Alphe

Dear Sir,

The word "repercussion" doesn't half say it.

This morning, we received in the mail 4,325 letters. We'd never seen so many. The director was beaming. He thought it was an avalanche of orders, and was already congratulating himself aloud on having written a brilliant circular which would stand the literary market on its ears. He came down a peg or two when we opened the letters. Among these 4,325 letters there were exactly four orders for *The Inca Adventure*, and 4,321 letters which expressed a most diverse variety of sentiments, ranging from cold anger to terror. A good many of our dear members wanted to know if we'd gone off our rockers. At the same time, we received 1,432 formal and irrevocable terminations of membership.

It amounted to an unprecedented panic. Nothing yet has happened in the world at large, but something *has* finally happened at the office. History's just revenge: for the world has witnessed many sensational events, while we at the office have invariably been left out. Now we are making up for lost time. And we're making up for it at a goodly pace. The eleven o'clock mail has dumped an additional 728 letters on our desks.

Strange . . . no one has yet guessed that a mere employee of this very office was the one responsible for slipping this "devil's handbill"—to quote one of our clients— in with the courteous Monthly Letter. All of them believe in some "outside" intervention. Malevolent, of course. The most absurd theories have first claim among the wealth of suppositions. Yet the mystery is so unmysterious.

No need to tell you that, this morning, there's no question of being bored at the office.

Very sincerely yours, with all my thanks,

J.S., DIRECTOR

THE ADVENTURE STORY BOOK CLUB/Paris

Paris, 9/6/55

Monsieur Strigel
Xeriac-sur-Alphe

Dear Sir,

The "repercussions" continue.

Your correspondents have kept their word. Throughout the world, the press is slowly learning about the mystery of the "Flier." Already, there are enormous headlines in this morning's papers. BLACK HUMOR? SIMPLE HOAX? some query. WHAT IF IT WERE TRUE? another asks.

As you predicted, skepticism has followed all the uproar. Specialists are obtaining these documents of the planet Agonese the Luminous. They are studying them. Their first statements are cautious, but they clearly perceive the immediate necessity of setting up a Commission of Enquiry, specially attached to the study of this brochure

which has already been designated as a "foreign object."
It is being submitted to exhaustive analysis, ink, paper,
fibers, literary composition, everything.

At the office, we have had to hurriedly engage a battal-
ion of secretaries. To date, we have gotten 13,658 letters.
And ten orders for *The Inca Adventure*. The Affair of the
Document has sent business figures plummeting.

I have been implored to reconsider my decision to quit.
I no longer write anything, I merely supervise. Among the
secretaries we've taken on, there are several who take
pleasure in my supervising them. There is so much work
to do before we can waste some time together. As for the
author of *The Inca Adventure*, he's bringing suit against
us. This explorer of the shrubbery of the Amazon believes
in terrestrial adventures. He believes *only* in them. He
denies the rest. He is preparing a lecture on the difference
between the butterflies of Upper Brazil and those of
Lower Guiana.

Very sincerely yours,

J.S., DIRECTOR

THE ADVENTURE STORY BOOK CLUB/Paris
Paris, 9/7/55

Monsieur Strigel
Xeriac-sur-Alphe

Dear Sir,

The whole world knows about it by now.
And the perplexity is universal.
The analyses have all been explicit. The paper of this
flier was not made on Earth, the ink is unknown to us, the
printing poses an unfathomable mystery. It has been

admitted that this flier really comes from a world called
Agonese the Luminous.

As for the little scientific problems in the flier, they appear in the eyes of all specialists as enigmas of an unknown
kind. In vain, they seek to resolve them; but they are con-
vinced this is, in no sense of the word, a joke.

Thousands of enquiries have been opened. They are attempting to ascertain how the fliers arrived from Xeriac-
sur-Alphe on Earth. There is one thing to be feared—
that certain correspondents, if questioned, will betray the
secret. But can this really be of importance?

Very sincerely yours,

J.S., DIRECTOR

Xeriac-sur-Alphe

Monsieur Gardère
The Adventure Story Book Club
Paris

Dear Sir,

This letter will doubtless be the last. After this, I will
have nothing more to say to you.

What you tell me concerning the repercussions brought
on by the brochure mailed throughout the world hardly
surprises me. It was foreseeable, and foreseen.

But the "sensation" for us is not contained in this fact.
Which, besides, in our eyes, has not the slightest importance. The "sensation" will only come later. Much later.

The text of the flier evidently excited you. There was, in
fact, no reason for it to. We might just as well have sent
you an advertisement for some hairdresser down there. The
essential was not, as you thought, to have you read some-

thing, but to have you touch something. That is to say, only the "material" of the flier really mattered.

This material contained a germ. Invisible to you, impossible to decompose chemically, perfect in fact. At present, tens of millions of Earthlings have touched these fliers. The germ entered them upon contact. You have all been infected. And you have infected all those around you, everyone whom you so much as brush against, everyone whom you will brush against in the future. No need to mention that it's impossible, with the means you possess, to do away with this germ. At your present stage, you would have to burn out all living and inert matter in your world. Even so, the germ would probably survive.

You will ask what the consequences of this germ will be. Rest assured, there's no danger. You will have been dead a long time before the consequences of this germ finally make themselves felt. But the die is cast. Two generations from now, the men of your planet will be reduced to a size much inferior to that which has been your lot for so many centuries. As a matter of fact, you're going to be dwarves. The tallest among you will not exceed a stature of 30 inches. The average height will be 25–26 inches. This is so. Such is the fate that awaits your grandchildren.

Why have we acted thus? As a game? For fun? Because we felt like it? Certainly not. I told you that my letters concealed a precise goal. I meant what I said.

It is, in fact, our intention to conquer your world some centuries from now. At that time, we will need it.

But, on the one hand, we have no wish to fight against powerful giants. And on the other hand, we want a world which will be immediately available without putting us to the trouble of useless transformations. Yours will be there for us. For, in one hundred and fifty years, you will have to entirely rebuild your world to your new measure.

You will have to reconstruct everything, re-create all, re-think each object. We prefer to leave you the chore of this slightly absurd endeavor. And so tedious. Can you see us, the conquerors of the Future, stooping to such mundane tasks as sawing the legs of tables or lowering doorknobs to a reasonable height?

I refer to our height.

For, as I told you, we have, like you, two eyes, a nose, a mouth, two arms. All this is true. But I forgot to mention a detail which will make everything clear to you: we are only 28 inches tall. No more. We regret this very much, of course.

But, as you can see, it will all work out quite well.

Very sincerely yours,

S. STRIGEL

THE
EPHEMERA

We were going to die.

This is not something very original, after all: everyone has to die one day. One day or another, sure. But we were going to die any hour now. That was the difference, and we knew it.

For some hours, in fact, we had lost control of our touring astrovessel. It was the first time that this had happened to me. And the last, of course. Yet I had navigated millions of miles in this machine, it was guaranteed for ten more years, and had been checked before my departure from Shell 45, a platform station moored in midspace, some millions of miles from Earth. We had spent the night there at the Esso Palace, rendezvous for all lovers of Galaxy S 43, desirous of spending the weekend at Treges-les-Sables, whose vast beaches of fine gold were still rather deserted, but already very well known.

You might say that our chances were much better for ending this weekend in the void: lost, we were adrift in space, at the mercy of its currents. There were two of us, Ylge and myself. I was trying not to think. She may have been thinking that she had always been told that it was dangerous to go off with someone you didn't know for a weekend. Especially when the stranger drove a rocket the way people once drove those wheezy convertibles, risking death at every tree, at speeds nonetheless ap-

proaching immobility. It's said that these old-time weekends killed many people. A risk that no longer exists:
there's no danger of collisions in space, where there is
room for everyone. Too much room in fact, which was
why we were heading for infinity, disoriented, engulfed.

That's where we were, i.e. nowhere, when I discovered
that world which was called Drige the Translucent. The
name had its charm, as did the world it represented. But
this world appeared in no tourist brochure, in no colorful
travel poster. According to the reports, Drige was a forbidden world. Landing there was prohibited.

A ridiculous prohibition: between certain death in space
and probable death on this world, it was not difficult to
choose the second alternative.

On the first contact with this world, I heaved a sigh of
relief: the air was breathable. Air, at last: air which didn't
come out of a tube. Air, and a faint, barely perceptible
breeze. It was gentle. Calm. And this world was silent.
It was also night, a sombre yet green darkness. By my
watch, it was 2 A.M.

As for the surface, it was neither quicksand nor carniv-
orous plants, as I might have feared. It was, on the contrary, mossy, singularly elastic, almost as springy as a
mattress.

"You're sure this planet is off limits?" Ylge asked me.

I was sure, unfortunately. I didn't know much of French
history, but I knew my Michelin by heart, and the name
Drige had been ticked off with three death's heads. Maca-
bre sign of great danger. As for knowing why. . . . But
our chances of finding out to our sorrow were very good.

Ylge stretched out on the ground. She was already
asleep. I let myself go, curling up beside her, throwing
caution to the wind. At any rate, I did not have the requi-
site capacities for detecting, among a thousand apparently

normal details, the invisible trap that might cost us our lives. And then, I was tired. After all, if one had to die, better to pass out in this velvety softness. And really, the ground, which seemed all feathers and warmth, smacked more of the bed than the tomb. I fell asleep with the very thought that bed and death often went together.

But what . . .

I woke up from my sleep as if I were back on Earth. A bit groggy and not exactly disposed to accomplish great feats.

The first thing I found astonished me was my watch. It read 2:05. I thought it had stopped. But I could see the second hand ticking around the dial. Ylge had just gotten up.

"I slept well," she said to me.

"You slept for two minutes," I told her.

"A century," she replied.

At that moment, I thought I could see how we might both be right. A minute, a century, it no longer signified. We were no longer on Earth. We were elsewhere, on a world which was unknown to us, on solid ground which was no doubt a mirage of security: in reality, it represented an abyss of unfathomable laws.

"I'm so thirsty," murmured Ylge.

I was thirsty, too. And hungry.

But the time had come, not to drink or eat, but to look, and see.

Since it was morning, there was something to see; and the landscape was well worth a glance. Indeed, it nearly gave me a shock—I who had seen other worlds, in all forms, and causing all degrees of stupefaction, since for my pleasure I'd taken to planet hopping around the universe.

Dazzled, I let the landscape of *this* planet sink into my mind.

Everything on Drige was transparent: explosions of light, sparkling fireworks, dazzlement. Such was the first impression that one registered. Then, one perceived that a single color underlay it all. This color was a very pale, almost grayish, green. As for the countless arabesque arrangements of this world, which one might have believed were formed of crystal, they were entangled, knotted with one another with such grace, such fluidity that it would have been impossible to separate what appertained to the plant world from that which was artificial, just as one saw no way at all to distinguish objects or isolated masses in this one mass which uttered but a single cry of light and fineness of form. A single network of tones in which no detail was allowed to stand out, a single labyrinth of transparencies whose lines and curves seemed to obey the laws of liquidity of a new geometry of elongation. Strictly speaking, one could make out an inextricable compromise, as if nature, on this world, had been able to join in love with the multiple variations of a civilization whose refinement could not be doubted.

Like myself, Ylge gazed on all this captivated. What could she say? What tourists say when they disembark at Mont St. Michel, or in the valley of the Chevreuse, or discover for the first time the subterranean ocean of Fourme-les-Neiges.

"Some landscape!" Ylge murmured.

I agreed. Thinking that if it was not prominently featured in all the agency brochures, but instead placed off limits, it was doubtless for good reasons. Reasons so unreassuring that I preferred not to think of them.

"Where are we?" Ylge asked.

I was asking this myself, with no success. I had always

laughed when I read twentieth century novels of the future, in which intrepid spacemen set their conquering feet on lands which they defined without even thinking about it: here a forest, there a city, there a Martian suburb; a tree here, and further on a telegraph pole, and even a streetlamp and a mailbox. One felt that they'd never left Nanterre. The reality proved very different. Most worlds were so strange to us that we lacked words to describe them, theorems to understand them, and imagination to acknowledge them.

Thus, on Drige the Translucent, we were completely lost in a maze of suppositions. We did not even know whether we'd landed in a Drigian city, or simply in open country. Anyone who could have said which would get a "genius" rating.

What must these sheer walls represent, that formed a barrier across the horizon? Architecture pure of ornament, mountains, a glass trap, the walls of a giant arena, cliffs? We didn't have the slightest idea. And this matter, which reminded one of glass, and was all around us: of what, exactly, was it made? We didn't know that either. What were these transparent tentacles that writhed in singular elegance, attaching themselves to seductive convulsions of curves and slender stems? Plants or subway entrances, decorative motifs or a tropical glade? No answer here either. And these silver puddles with which the ground was dotted at regular intervals? How was one to take them? As picturesque little lakes? Certainly not, for this silvery surface was not water. Mirrors? Mouths of sewers? Spots, placed there by an artist who had considered the whole planet as a canvas for an abstract painting? Absurd? Not more so than other hypotheses, nor less. Besides, more remarkable things have been seen in the universe than an abstract planet painting, certainly.

Also, because we had seen a full range of horrors, we knew that the most dangerous planets were not necessarily those which opened under your feet or spit dragon flames at the sight of a living being. Often, the most treacherous ones were exactly those which at first sight seemed welcoming and still. Like Drige, in fact. Drige the Tricky. We could only ask ourselves which incomprehensible detail of this world was going to reveal itself as an aggressor, and how things would turn out. We were also well aware of the wealth of choices that lay before us. It might take the form of a brutal oxidation of our organs upon contact with the ground, as on Trychnos, a veritable graveyard where ten Earth divisions met death on the field of horror. The radiations of this luminous transparence might prove fatal, as on Grammos 4, whose deadly secret our chemists were vainly attempting to fathom. At the stroke of noon, the planet might emit a sudden uproar, whose sharp sounds would literally tear us apart, as happened to those who had arrived as pioneers on Thurge. Or the reflections, when the sun was fully risen, might prove as murderous as they are on Yglege, a planet which appears from afar as a ball of mica, bristling with plates like so many mirrors. Short of supposing that on Drige, as on Spondyle, there existed a system of treacherous underground swamps, and that at a certain hour, without warning, the landscape of solid mass would turn into a single clinging marsh, enough to swallow us up like a couple of mere pebbles.

I was randomly sorting out these bits and ends of memories, when Ylge took me by the arm.

"Listen," she said.

From the bowels of the earth, there arose an indistinct melody, like a formless *purée* of sounds in which had been blended a multitude of infinitely melancholy plaints.

"This world's inhabited," Ylge commented. "It's better that way, don't you think?"

"It depends on what inhabits it," I answered.

But we had no thoughts of fleeing, or of hiding ourselves. Flight, we knew, might cost us our lives in a landscape whose snares and invisible abysses we were ignorant of. Hide ourselves? Where, in a world that was completely transparent?

Then, something appeared, something living.

"Look," said Ylge, "a fish."

A long shape, covered with scales that glittered in the sun, emerged from the depths of one of the pools that dotted the ground. It came out with an extreme slowness, traversing the silver surface as if it were not a material thing, but simply a color. If it was a fish, it was a flying fish, because it was now hovering above the ground; always slowly, as if it were rising under terrible pressure, yet with considerable grace and ease. Needless to say, this slowness was natural to it, obviously so. We watched the fish open out its scales, saw it lengthen, so that we took it for a serpent, until we realized that this creature with silver scales was in reality but an arm. And this arm belonged to a being that was emerging *in toto* from the pool.

Drige was indeed an inhabited world. From all the silvery pools that lay around us, living creatures were emerging. They all moved with such *lenteur* that we developed eyestrain following their heavy, sluggish movements. They all resembled each other and, in fact, were rather like us. Like us, they had four limbs, a torso and a head, but filiform; they were clearly larger than us, and their arms seemed strangely elongated, evoking rather vividly the hind legs of praying mantises. From head to toe they were sheathed in coats of woven mail, very fine;

and they seemed to be actually glazed with scales, like our fish. Of their face, if they had one, there was nothing visible but enormous, globular eyes, of a luminous red so bright that it was as if they had light bulbs in their skulls.

There we were, in front of them, and nothing happened. They did not advance towards us; they dragged themselves along in a strangely indolent way. But most of them remained immobile, hieratic. Sometimes they communicated among themselves. In a language which appeared to be a melody composed of sounds as prolonged as their movements. A soft, liquid language that conveyed no barbarisms, no harshness.

"Either they don't see us, or they really don't care," Ylge remarked.

"You'd think so. They don't hear us either."

"Do you think it's a trick, or what?"

"Why would they bother to set a trap for us? They outnumber us. And they seem to be armed. Look . . ."

One of the creatures was advancing, pointing at the sky with a long glass spear that branched into several fine barbs, artfully worked. He, or *it*, was advancing towards us, and its slowness now chilled my blood. Nevertheless, the eyes did not seem to be looking at us. I stepped in front of Ylge, took out my gun, and was ready to shoot.

"It's long . . . it's terrible," murmured Ylge.

It *was* long, in fact. The Drigian was advancing no faster than a snail; it was scarcely moving. I was about to fire when I thought to turn around, and saw the prey which the Drigian had in view. A few feet above the ground, as languorous as the humanoids of this world, glided a sort of medusa of the airs, sweeping the length of its transparent filaments in algaelike motions. From the Drigian's pike there darted a blinding light, and the medusa was flung between the prongs of the weapon, inert, as if petrified. The way it looked there, one could have sworn that it was part of the weapon, simply one of its arabesques.

"A hunter," said Ylge.

"You're right. The equivalent of our undersea fishing. Everything has its counterpart in nature."

Another fact seemed obvious. We truly did not exist for them.

"They won't be the ones who kill us," I said.

"But we're going to die just the same?" asked Ylge.

I believed so, yes. Something told me, I didn't know what. I seemed to feel death already within me. It was not exactly rambling around us in the shape of these creatures, but was already inside us. Perhaps it was the hunger and the thirst that I felt more and more sharply turning their knife in my throat and belly. Or the fatigue. How was it possible to believe that we had just slept, and had eaten plenty the night before? Once more, I looked at my watch. Not possible, surely, but it was only 2:06. And I felt as if I were dropping with fatigue, and as if I had eaten nothing for at least several days. It was then that Ylge asked me when I had shaved.

"What?"

"When did you shave?"

As I recalled, it had been just before landing on this world. I told her so.

"Give me your hand," said Ylge.

She took it, and rubbed it against my jaw. It gave me a shock.

"You would think it was at least four or five days since you had shaved."

Four or five days, one could have sworn on it. And my hunger. And our thirst. And on this world, for this world, barely five minutes had elapsed.

Then I understood.

I understood it all. The extreme slowness with which these creatures moved. Their immobility. The fact that they did not see us. That they did not hear our voices. That we did not exist for them.

"The time, Ylge; it's the time."

"The time?"

"Yes. There's an asynchronism. We are not living in their time. We are in their space, but not in their time."

"But we see them."

"Us, yes. Them, no. We are nothing for them. A fugitive gleam, perhaps, a flash. We are living too fast for their perception. But we are nonetheless subject to the law of this world."

"The law?"

"Yes. The most dangerous one. Five minutes have passed for the inhabitants of Drige, but for us, several days of our time have passed. It is several days already since we've had anything to eat or drink. And we are also dead tired."

"We can sleep, can't we?"

Yes, this we could. But doubtless that is all we could. And sleep might well kill us if we went without eating. There was some question on this food subject, but not much. It seemed to me obvious that this world contained not a crumb of anything that would be suitable for us as food. And nowhere had I seen the slightest trace of so much as a drop of water. This thought led to another. I suddenly remembered the page on Drige in my Michelin guide. I saw in my mind the words Drige The Translucent in capitals followed by three death's heads, and I saw just as clearly the printed phrase: a world where it never rains. A world without water. We were not facing our death yet, but we were facing the fact that would cause it. And where could we find help? Who was there to call? A desert, I thought. We were lost in a desert. We were in the heart of a civilization, among a group of individuals who were perhaps ready to assist us, but our situation was hardly more enviable than that of a ship wrecked on a deserted shore. And each minute that passed was doubtless equivalent to hours of privation, hours which were bringing us certain death . . .

A spasm of rebellion shook me. There was no question of digging with my teeth in the soil of a world without water or plants; but I could at least try to get the attention of this world's inhabitants. The hunter was there before me. He would need more time than this to get away. A few minutes would hardly be enough for him to turn around. In a single leap, with all my weight, I tackled him around the legs, as if I were trying to down a rugby player. But the Drigian didn't so much as budge. There was no reaction. Evidently, I had had the same effect on him as a feather falling on myself would have. I really was nobody in this world. We were nothing. Still alive, but already no longer anything.

Ylge had slumped to the ground. She seemed exhausted. I went to her. I touched her, letting my head rest between her thighs. It was good there. The need to make love tormented me for a moment. But this was already no more than an abstract desire: an act beyond my strength.

"What are they doing, over there?" murmured Ylge.

I turned to look at them. Most of the Drigians appeared absorbed in some labor which I tried in vain to define. At any rate, they moved with such extreme slowness that, strictly speaking, their acts, whatever they might be, seemed devoid of meaning. Nonetheless, one fact became clear: by some kind of magic imperceptible to us, they were provoking subtle variations in the fluorescent landscape that lay around us. Games of light and metamorphoses that came into play, only to dissolve and re-create themselves. Masses were changing form; others disappeared, as if inexplicably erased from reality. Contours lengthened, twisting themselves about, always in slow motion. Within the matter itself there were silent explosions of light, passing from tube to tube with the grace of a jet of steam. And from these variations were born sounds as moving as the forms that breathed them forth in this climate of ideal indolence, as if each detail of this world had been endowed with a perfection long since achieved.

An abstract sculpture? One could well have believed it. These beings seemed to constitute a single band of impassive artisans, playing at throwing into space the useless and changing arabesques of a sculpture ever rebegun. Or perhaps they were devoting their efforts to some incomprehensible experiment of a science alien to our logic. Unless we had simply landed in an office where practical accounting was performed with symbols that we took, wrongly, as the manifestations of a refined art. Or an open-air factory perhaps, a factory literally set in the landscape, constituted of machines impossible to distinguish from the natural decor? And in a few minutes we would see the Drigians mass-produce knitting needles, slices of ham, or double crepe soles.

I looked, I tried to understand. But already a curtain of fog had descended between what I saw and my capacity for reasoning. My mind seemed to become macerated, and to dissolve. The fog was composed of the hunger, thirst, and, fatigue that parched my throat with its density.

Somewhere between magic and nightmare. I thought of this, confusedly. That is exactly where we were. Enchantment was there, around us, sparkling, so calm and reassuring, in a world where all was luminous, calm and slow, and filled with refined luxury and softness. The night-mare was in ourselves, and it was impossible to escape, to flee and take refuge in the enchantment that served as decor. A decor as futile as a mirage. Or perhaps not; perhaps we were the mirages. Living mirages. In this world, for those who inhabited this world, we were noth-ing but invisible, abstract objects. A mirage, if you will. . . . Suddenly deranged, I wanted to act, strike, shout, tear into pieces this barrier which . . .

I didn't even succeed in standing up; I collapsed, com-pletely done in. I had the impression of having wandered for days and days along an endless corridor. I could do no more.

I crept up to one of the long needles in the landscape —the spine of a Drigian cactus, or simply a retort of their motorless equipment—how could I tell? I wanted to break it, scratch it, tear it out, to destroy something in this world, and make myself noticed, or perhaps provoke some short circuit, force these creatures to register our presence. I tried desperately, but in vain. Nothing gave. This trans-parency, evocative of crystal, had the solidity of tem-pered steel. Then I shouted, again in vain. I fell back, drenched in sweat. I felt Ylge's hand, caressing my cheek. A hand clammy with its last moisture, already the hand of a corpse. A dead hand touching a dead person.

"We shouldn't have done it," I murmured.

"There was nothing else to do," said Ylge.

I thought I could hear Ylge say good-night, then noth-ing.

When I tried to awaken Ylge, I realized that she would never wake again.

I had met her the week before. Yes, just the week be-fore. Her kindness had immediately touched me. More, even, than the contours of her body or the beauty of her face.

"I'd like very much to go on a weekend trip with you," she had said. "After that, we'll see."

So. And now, we'd seen everything. And I, myself, was seeing *her* for the last time. She already looked so blurred, so far, and yet so near, so indistinct.

But an uproar assaulted my ears, making me leap to my feet.

First, there was a single flash of light that enveloped the entire landscape. And, as if it had been gravely burned, the whole landscape emitted a strange cry of sorrow, or of triumph. I then saw the Drigians slowly approach a certain place, and form a circle around something liquid that was flowing, flowing transparently, so pure, so common, so colorless in this green-tinted maze.

Water, no doubt.

Water was what the Drigians were making. Nothing else. The water I'd been dreaming of in the depths of my throat, in the bottom of my gut.

"Water," I murmured.

I wanted to get up, move, speak, cry, plunge into the water, but these acts were far beyond me. I fell forward, staring blindly at the water, which just kept on flowing.

It was only then that the Drigians perceived the two Earthlings.

Death had caused them to enter their temporal space. The immobility of death.

They approached the two bodies. They touched them. Then, without clearly understanding, or knowing what to do, they went to get water.

And with infinite gentleness, they gave water to the corpses.

VACATION

Since its annexation in 2012, the planet has been called Azur Bis. This planet of two suns truly had all the advantages: a dreamlike climate, golden cliffs and silvery sands, limpid water, and a relaxing absence of all forms of animal life. It was in September 2013 that the planet swallowed, in a single gulp, the 500,000 tourists who had come to spend their vacations there. The planet possessed no other life than its own: it alone was alive here, and it savored living beings.

But it liked them tanned, sleek with the wind and summer, warm and well cooked.

Now that we are in it, up to our necks, it has to be admitted that they were all wrong in their predictions. The incurable pessimists as well as the optimists, no less incurable surely. Some had, in fact, predicted that the Atomic Era would usher in the end of the world, others that it would be synonymous with a Golden Age of Happiness for all.

Whom must we believe? In reality, the world is still here, nearly intact, and the gold is still buried in bank vaults, just as "happiness" is still a myth with which Chiefs of State and sociologists spice their discourses and theories. And yet, the Atomic Era has been in full swing for a long time now. It has been an age of every conceivable triumph and apotheosis; the most spectacular surprises lay in wait for us. But these abstract advantages aside, what have we gained on the level of the everyday, of reality? Simply an increase in boredom, with new little worries, new taxes, and a formidable increase in the cost of living. And also, innumerable sources of temptation, which make of our lives an exhausting chase after material things, after the many improvements which are constantly being made. A chase after money, in fact, since many things have been replaced, but nothing has replaced money or the essential laws of business. And money is more than ever synonymous with forced labor. In other words, we have done nothing but amplify the raving madness which has held the world in its grip since the invention of the car and electricity. More than ever, the act of earning a living resembles an act of damnation.

That life has become an interminable process of addition interspersed with various operations, with subtractions in particular, and that it unfolds in a single explosion of bills, no one can any longer doubt. And from year to year things get worse and become more critical.

It seems that in the twentieth century household gas, fuel, coal, or electricity were a major part of the budget; but how can one compare the price of these primitive materials with the towering bills for atomic energy which we are forced to use, and which soon devours the better part of any salary? Not to mention that all equipment nowadays runs on atomic energy. Even the potato strainer, the alarm clock, and (who knows) perhaps our very hearts. Taxes were heavy in the past also, it seems, but then, at least, one could be out of work or penniless. Not so now: everyone makes a big salary, and the taxes are correspondingly big. We are wallowing in opulence and prosperity. So much so that we're even made to pay for the air which we breathe in our apartments. The air meters are everywhere, and the man of the twenty-second century, if like his ancestors he always has one foot in the grave, is living on the other on a grand footing, incessantly haunted by the desire to make a lot, and spend more.

The era of small apartments, pedestrians, idlers, and people content with their humble lot belongs to an age as distant as that of the serfs or combats of slaves in the arena. Now, everyone has to have standing. More than ever, people are bent on impressing each other. Normally, a person nowadays has his *pied-à-terre* in the city where he works, his mansion in the suburbs, and a villa by the sea, or in the mountains, or on some countrified planet. He must possess two cars, one for the city, where the speed limit is twenty miles an hour, the other for the highway, where one may sometimes exceed forty miles an hour if the traffic is not too intense. Almost always he owns an outboard, since the departmental canals are often less crowded than the roads. It would be more futile than ever to list all the electronic perfections, the hi-fi sets, the wall decorations, or little marvels of household art incrusted in the walls of every apartment. It would be impossible to count them, but no one can now do without them. One doesn't even dream of doing without them. No need, either, to mention the fact that these machines cost a fortune, and that, *richesse oblige*, they are accordingly taxed. A vicious circle in which people are running blindly, lost, distracted, drunk on running faster without any exact idea of what they are looking for.

As for the essential law of existence, it has undergone almost no change: if you want to buy, you need money;

and money, like health, comes from work.

Work that is suited to an era where all that counts is the extreme sophistication, the unfathomable subtlety of a science moving forward, always in gestation. For a long time now, there has been no question of being interested in one's work, or taking it seriously, but simply of doing it. Like in the past, when they sent you to break stones in forced labor. Every job, even the humblest, is intimately connected with electronics, and is such a maze of complexities that only computer brains can understand what the humans are mindlessly performing. People are no longer asked to think, but to prove their efficiency, to produce. In history, man has always been a beast of burden; at present, he is a beast of algebraic burden. He has gained nothing in the process, if not a brutalization even greater than in the past, and a continual migraine which, happily, science has learned to mitigate by mixing aspirin in all food sold on the market. But, aside from these preventive measures, it has still been found necessary to modify the classic schedules which had been in effect since the twentieth century. To have but one day of rest per week and three weeks' vacation a year subjected people to a régime of overwork, which for many years kept psychoanalysts and private asylums in business. In the face of this state of affairs, which was steadily worsening, the authorities resigned themselves to changing the existing schedules, although they were all the more practical for being rigorous. They changed everything. Thus, for the past ten years already, throughout the world, after five days of work there has been a five-day vacation. Then one starts again. It is the universal law. On the other hand, the working day is fifteen hours, with a short break after three hours, a mandatory drug at six to keep going. And, willy-nilly, one does keep going.

This is how I have lived for thirty-five years in this world. I'm not about to congratulate myself. But what can I do about it? It's only the science fiction writers who, for three centuries, have been talking with puerile perseverance about voyages through time. Mirage, mirage. Up to now, no one has succeeded in leaving this century. In a sense, it's lucky, since if an organized departure for the future or the past were to occur, tourist class or even first class, very few people would remain in this insane century.

One must, then, accept things as they are, acknowledging that one cannot really change them. There remains, by way of consolation, that gift of resignation which we inherit from our most distant ancestors, and the little proverbs which the inventive spirit of man has created for himself. Such is life. Where there's life, there's hope. One must put up with it. As one makes one's bed, so one lies in it. And so on. Little steps, little phrases of resignation, from the cradle to the grave. And, whether one lived before Christ or under Charlemagne, in the nineteenth century or in the twenty-second century, they have never prevented anyone from dying. What's the use of living well when one always has to die badly. None of this is worth even the trouble of trying to dream up some change of principle. Better not to think too much about it, and take things as they come.

And smile, for example, since today I am off. Five days of rest to spend in the high-fidelity uproar of Music-to-Relax-By, or some massive traffic jam, or the aggressively variegated explosion of thousands of leisure shows which descend like harpies on the salary holders of the world. Unless one decides to take off for another world of one's choice. A calm world, since the human fuss has not yet spread to all corners of the universe. I think about it, and it seems to me a provisional solution, banal certainly, but acceptable. And I shouldn't forget that it's been a good fifteen days since I last left Earth, and my health is suffering for it. A change of air could only do me good.

Having decided, the rest is simply a matter of routine. One proceeds to the proper places, follows the guides and directional signs which litter this world, keeps on paying, and everything works smoothly; the planet has, within itself, an administrative machinery so well oiled that even disorder is subtly organized, ready to go, primed.

Having eaten a one-price breakfast so as not to lose time, I go to the Pook Agency (Other Worlds Department, Third Floor) where, in a setting of mobiles and changing light patterns, the harmonies of an eternal sidereal concert encourage the uncertain to take the plunge.

"*What can I do for you?*" asks the young woman who welcomes me, speaking English. She's aware that for many years now Americans have been traveling more frequently than others.

I'm surprised, nonetheless: I'm not wearing my foreign tie this morning.

"I should be glad to look at some brochures," I tell her, partly in English, so as not to break the news too abruptly that English is only my *father* tongue.

"How would you like to see them?" she asks solicitously. "On full color TV? In hi-fi 3 D? In odorascope? Or perhaps you'd prefer to hear them in one of our listening booths."

"Just brochures will do, thanks."

The young woman hands me a bundle of brochures with the expression of those who distrust easily accommodated clients, disinclined to avail themselves of the most modern devices. It must be said that very few people are still willing to read anything at all, when sound and image are the rule everywhere. I'm amazed, leafing through the brochures. What a choice! Since man has conquered the stars, the choice of trips offered by the agencies has acquired proportions that seem to defy human imagination. Where to go? The most difficult part is still making up one's mind. But to stay on Earth when I have five days off seems slightly absurd to me.

I try to make a choice, to see clearly, but after a few seconds the possibilities put me in a torpor. Above all, I see colors, for technicolor has invaded this world so completely that I ask myself if the night is still black and white. And the glossy paper of the brochures, as well as the four-color illustrations, often flatters certain landscapes which turn out to be rather less prepossessing than they appeared in full-page spreads. Not to mention the worlds where I've already been, and have no wish to see again. I look, I touch the pages in relief, I snuff up the olfactory-sensitive landscapes; I try to dream, create for myself enchanting mirages, but in vain. To give dreams a chance, you have to believe that the reality is unattainable. This is evidently not the case: nothing is unattainable, not even the impossible. I shall have to decide quickly, though, since most of the rockets leave between noon and one.

May as well forget about planet K.02, where, at this very moment, atomic experiments are being carried out as part of major spring manoeuvres. T.23 brings to mind last year's dismal vacation in a gray, milky wind, sugary and gentle, and so opaque that to this day I ask myself if this world had a landscape or not. U.1 seems more alluring as I read the prospectus, but only t.b. patients are allowed to go there. The appeal of G.34 is no less great, and I might indeed be tempted, except that Paramount has had the brainstorm of transforming this world into a permanent spectacle: Sound, Odor, and Light. Racism prevails on O.8, and whites aren't admitted. And you have to wait for winter to go to H.54, since the larvae of this planet secrete a spittle in springtime that inundates the entire landscape.

Better still to take counsel with the employee who seems to be in hibernation under the sign Information in a little glass cage. I place myself in front of the microphone, and put my questions to her slowly and clearly.

"I would like to take an extraterrestrial vacation, but I have to be back in five days."

Without opening her eyes or changing expression, almost without moving, she somnambulistically consults a schedule and a map of the heavens.

"There *is* R.4, which is only a few million miles away from earth, but you have only ten seconds to catch the 12:30 rocket."

"That's not time enough?"

"I'm afraid not. There is also R.33, where the artificial heating is very agreeable at this time of year, but there is no return rocket before next week."

"How about F.04?"

"Unfortunately, that planet has been dropped from the catalogue. Its exact location has been a mystery for the past few days. If you were to ask me, I'd say M.77 . . ."

"I hear it's very cold there."

"Not so cold. . . . If you're warmly dressed, you can take a bath there any time you like."

None of this seems very tempting to me. I'm on the point of asking myself why I don't simply stay on Earth, and go to one of the beaches of the Arthritic Ocean, which for twenty years has submerged Arizona. Unless I buy a ticket for P.4, a planet which I know well, since I spent all my vacations there as a child. So be it. Why not?

I arrive on P.4 in late afternoon, after an uneventful

flight; and it is with some emotion that I see again the little summer house by the hill which has belonged to my family for two generations. I know that I will always find it in perfect condition, immaculate, since nothing ever changes on P.4, a world without dust, slag, or microbes. The colors themselves remain as they are, seasonless, a wash of hues so discreet that one might think them transparent. Colors in harmony with a nature of moss and sparkling sand, crystalline needles and velvety things, countless sprigs that glitter in the sun of this world like the scintillating parts of a gigantic crystal chandelier. As for the air, it's never troubled by a breeze, and the water does not have the density of a bubble; it falls in torrential, noiseless cascades, half liquid, half gas. Life is slow and easy on this world, without tornadoes, storms, or cataclysms. And the Translucides, who dwell in troops on this planet, are no less placid.

Oviparous, multivorous, strangoloid, no doubt apostalitic, menocene, but for all that argigorous, the Translucides are tall biped medusae, lacking definite consistency, semi-immaterial, depending on the temperature, and extremely malleable. One could even swear that their sole activity is to slowly change form. Their one aim in life is to survive, which is easy, since there are no enemies to conquer, no obstacles to surmount. And in a climate of extreme languor, they methodically devour their planet, and their enormous languid eyes express a permanent, singularly insistent despair. They do not speak; they utter their complaint in a single bass note, always the same. Their entire civilization appears to be contained in this note of distress, this eternal reproach, evidently addressed to the sky.

Since P.4 contains neither precious metals nor natural resources, and since nothing there can be commercially

exploited, not even the disincarnated texture of the Translucides, men have never thought to make a colony of this
world, just as it has never occurred to them to place the
Translucides under a terrestrial protectorate. What could
they do with creatures who spend an hour or two swallow-
ing a single leaf, and who, moreover, can make themselves
completely invisible if need be? That is why, on P.4, one
meets only a few scattered vacationers in this backwater
of the universe.

Nonetheless there are, as everywhere in the universe,
certain drawbacks to P.4. First of all, the nights.

Indeed, if the days are steeped in calm ennui, the nights
seem to belong to a twinging nightmare, cunningly staged,
harmless of course, but rather difficult to bear.

The night, here, is the baffling scene of fluctuations,
imponderables, and subtle metamorphoses. Mirages? Hal-
lucinations? Apparitions? It has never been ascertained
which, but from the moment the sun sets, the formless
and the impalpable prevail. Colors drip through the air
inside of houses, bubbles of blood burst at floor level,
gaunt stems slowly push out from the ceiling. The walls
fill with rustling noises, as if millions of termites were
gathering there; the silence is broken by cries impossible
to define, shouting mirages, phantasmic gleams that engage in viscous struggles with moving forms. And in this
nightmare, the most disquieting role is that played by
the Translucides, who perform feats at night, by means
unknown to themselves, no doubt, such as they never do
in broad day. They go through walls, enter under the
doors, vanish in thin air, only to recompose themselves a
little later. When I wake in the night, I always find a
number of Translucides about me, in frozen attitudes, or
elongated, like some agonized octopus. In the dark, they
are luminous or simply translucent, and I can watch them
stray across my bed, along the walls or ceiling, hair-rais-

ing yet peaceable, like soft fishbowls in which one can follow every movement of their larval organs. Sometimes they stretch out beside me, flat out like enormous puddles of milk. Touching them, you think of marble smeared with glue. In general, when I open my eyes I encounter the gaze, only inches away, of their enormous liquid eyes, so soft, and therefore all the more disquieting. And in the night, their monochord lament becomes a single, continuous moan, like that of a dog when it has been run over. It takes discipline to hear them without terror. To watch the Translucides grow flaccid, losing shape as they moan, and turning color as they will, now and again, from a ghastly pallor to green, is not so agreeable, either. Sometimes I tell myself that to stand these nights with a mob of larval, disconsolate phantoms, one must truly feel great love for a world like P.4.

A love no doubt hard to explain since, after all, even the days aren't so agreeable on P.4 where, strictly speaking, there are no distractions. Of course, it might be refreshing to take baths in the bubbly, vaporous waters of the yellow cascades; but I happen to know that the water of P.4 takes off your skin as it evaporates. It would be extremely tempting, also, to roll in the silvery sand of the high dunes; but consider the risk: the sand of this world attacks the flesh as aggressively as a horde of red ants. It would be no less intoxicating to run through the flaming savannahs of the plain, if the tall grasses didn't cut like razors, besides secreting some subtle venom.

My one distraction, in fact, is to relax in the doorway of my summer house, and tell myself that it would be nice to live here, that the landscape truly has its charm, and that the Translucides, with their parasitical sluggishness, are without question creatures easy to live with, and boon companions.

And then, what a rest cure, even if it *is* almost impossible to sleep at night, even if there's nowhere to lie down. But such reprieves must end. After four days, the vacation draws to a close, and I must think about returning to Earth in order to be in the office tomorrow morning.

At the P.4 base, then, I board the 3:30 rocket which will arrive on Earth by evening. There are only three of us, but already, to make up for lost time, we're crammed with soft music, advertising slogans, information, instructions, and news pictures. No doubt about it, we're returning to normal life.

"Have a nice flight," says the space hostess, whose sole function is to dole out courtesy phrases.

A wish unfulfilled, at any event, since an unexpected shock is in store for us on the return trip. Just as we are leisurely rounding T.43, one of the navigators announces, with the most perfect indifference, that we have deviated from the planned trajectory, and are doomed, for a year, to circle T.43, of which we have become an artificial satellite. Which brings us back to the inconveniences of planet hopping.

I say nothing, more resigned than the other two passengers, one of whom is due to become a father in a few days, while the other is beginning to shout that no one in his company will be able to balance the books this month without him. But raising your voice is not enough to counteract the inexorable laws of space.

"We will remain in touch with Earth," the navigator says to reassure us. We will receive supplies, fuel, and even mail. But we will not be able to land for a year. That's the way it is.

I should have brought some books. It's true that we have TV, high-fidelity advertising, technicolor, and other unpleasant artifacts of a civilization so far away and yet so near. A civilization which is thinking of us, for on the very next day I receive a cable from my office. It's explicit: "Regret to learn that you are held up in space. Will send work to you regularly. Make effort to write more legibly than usual. Obliged nonetheless to dock you a day's pay."

It's so reassuring! The world has not forgotten us.

And in fact, a day later, I receive, under seal, an important bundle of documents to study before feeding them to the electronic machines which devour them in an uproar of commercial gluttony. Truly, one would think oneself on Earth. And what joy to see, once more, the letterhead of the firm which employs me, its motto and its stylized eagle that seems to be breathing deeply in the pride of flying so high in the sky. By the same post, I have also received several bills, and the regular charges for instruments of higher than fifteen watts' power. One must not lose heart. We are far from the Earth, but near our creditors. And our employers are thinking of us.

Tomorrow, I'll no doubt get a list of indirect levies on reduced tax properties, then one of direct levies on local taxes. Then the monthly duty on the rural car which has been driven more than ten thousand miles. And the credit tax for the regularization of contract payments relative to certain receipts for noncommercial professions, with higher rates for all altitudes higher than twenty thousand miles. And so on. It's true that I will receive my salary at the end of the month, minus any bonuses for attendance, of course.

As for the rent which the company that owns this rocket will charge us, it's bound to be high. Not to mention the security and space taxes which we will have to assume.

A hard year lies ahead, even if our position is high. We will have to work day and night to pay for all this. But what can you do? This rocket has gotten lost in the sky. It might have been worse: we might have been condemned to circle this planet forever. Such is life. It goes on. More than this is necessary to escape it. Let's listen instead to its reassuring murmur. The radio has already informed us that a tornado has claimed twenty-five thousand victims in Japan; that a violent anti-Earth demonstration has broken out on G.87, where war is imminent; and that the secret of youth lies in regularly using Colgate toothpaste.

Well, we'll die as Earthlings, that's for sure, even if it happens far from our dear country. No one escapes his fate.

FUTURE
WITHOUT
FUTURE

In a world where it was impossible for a human being to distinguish between life and inanimate things, just as it was to differentiate the confused elements of the soil, the men committed an error which cost the lives of an entire landing squad.

Charmed by the dazzling orchestration of plants that burst open into a crystalline landscape, a biologist cut a plant of astonishingly bright reflection, and placed it in a glass of water.

It was this act that led to their undoing.

It was no plant that the biologist had plucked from the soil. It was the warrior-chieftain of this world.

In 1975, the world witnessed an event unique in history: a war ended for lack of combatants.

Faced, in fact, with the refusal to fight on the part of all American soldiers, they had had to stop the war in Vietnam. Even the career officers, the Marines, and the paratroopers had thrown down their arms, announcing their disgust and their decision to no longer take part in the massacre.

The news was as if an atomic bomb had been dropped. With the difference that the dropping of the bomb had seemed a much less alarming incident in the eyes of this planet's leaders. The Pentagon examined the situation in a stupor, understanding nothing. The Heads of State held a summit meeting, gravely shook their heads and, after several days of debate, decided to officially confirm that something must have changed in the world since World War I.

Nineteen hundred and seventy-five marked a date, spectacular certainly, but simply that of a beginning. Many others were to follow.

Many others, yes. It's not easy to speak about them. In the torrent of noisy events and underground stirrings of a *fin de siècle* which has never before so well deserved its name, how does one render exactly the fire and the ice, the explosive detail, and the slyly invisible current? How does one follow a precise chronology in a world where the notion of years, months, hours, and the calendar have gradually been lost? There's only one way to avoid the snare of dubious metaphysics or the sociology of vulgarization: to be content with jotting down some feverish notes, points of reference, burning observations, without trying to classify or analyze them so as to extract from them a definitive history of humanity. At any rate, there are no specialists left to write such a history.

Perhaps the sickness of the century, the beginning of the end, the fatal bug, was simply the disease of youth. Reassuring irony: this time, at least, the beginning truly *was* a *beginning*. Since the 1970's, youth had gotten itself talked about, and the uproar which it occasioned became, as time went by, a permanent storm. Not only had the younger generation been in the limelight for a long while, but it regularly filled page one in all newspapers. Even television, the race results, the household arts, and the problems of traffic had eventually been relegated to page two. And the more you discussed it, the more inextricably you became mired in it. It was no longer possible to doubt that youth intended to burn all its bridges without building new ones. It wished to know nothing of our past, of the future that lay ahead, of the stinking present being offered to it on a rusty plate. Each year consolidated the wall of concrete that rose between the two generations. The new refused to follow the old, and scarcely talked to it. Those who had turned twenty in 1965 were now approaching thirty, but curiously they had not capitulated, had not gone to work in their father's bank, or their uncle's factory. They did nothing, living off their relatives or their parents, sullen and silent, and secretly delighted to see their elders grow as agitated as shrimps in trying to support them. The schoolchildren of 1975 didn't wait for their twelfth birthday to become bored with the world, and reject possessions. As for the college students of 1975, they cultivated a lassitude and indifference so intense that even politics or movies had ceased to arouse them. Vis-à- vis the traditional working majority, this new generation represented a formidable force for inertia, a gigantic human mass whose age ranged from eleven years of age to thirty-five, and sometimes even beyond. In brief, their number was growing, and hope was diminishing. Useless to delude oneself; a terrible malady had contaminated this generation: lucidity. Miracles to the contrary, this time religion could do nothing for men. Even the religion of money, fame, and success left them cold. Neither publicity, nor specious promises, nor worldly arguments were enough to make them act. What, then?

Nineteen hundred and seventy-eight. In the chaos and confusion of its decade, this date is memorable. It is a date to be inscribed in gold, for all time. In this year, an official census reveals findings that terrify the promoters, authorities, and big worriers of production: throughout the world students have almost all abandoned their studies: they are content to know how to read and write, and the rest leaves them absolutely cold. To work, take a job, make a place for onself interests them even less. They aren't even really unemployed; they survive, without looking any farther. They find this world so absurd, so uproariously vulgar and stupid, that they wish to know nothing more about it, and want nothing more from it. They are absolutely uninterested in what happens or doesn't happen on this planet. This is frightening: if this goes on, who will take the baton, carry the torch of a civilization whose mark of quality is no longer much to brag about? Decimated more and more surely by pollution and the general insanity, the elders and working fathers are dying younger and younger, leaving holes that no one thinks of filling any more. There are scarcely enough persons to fill the gaps in companies. Some gaps close in about the ruins of a business: small enterprises and modest firms are failing for lack of successors in the family or among relations. Firms which were sailing on the sea of fortune, with the wind of prosperity behind them, are going down lock, stock, and barrel because no one wants to take the helm. The word "career" no longer means anything to a young person of twenty or twenty-five. Responsibilities bore them, so do schedules, and restraint even more so. They don't like to control, any more than they like being controlled. And the doctors search in vain for some ambition vitamin or faith pill to give the numberless misfits of this century. They want nothing to eat, nothing to drink, not even coffee, which stimulates them to no purpose, or drugs, which they gave up long ago.

The latter cost too much, and enrich gangsters, trusts, and governments, everything that they detest above all. In short, they see clearly. What can be done, on this planet, with a new breed that sees things, judges them, and politely puts them in the past? Above all, what can be done when this breed comes of age, and in time becomes the majority? Not so much the Silent Generation as the Refusing Generation.

The commercial panic is imperceptibly but ineluctably gaining ground. The consumer society is falling apart, exhausted. Bit by bit, investigations and inquiries are revealing facts which seem difficult to believe, but which prove to be quite undeniably true. All magazines devoted to the cult of woman, or to household objects, cars, house and garden equipment, knitting, or love horoscopes, have seen their clientele decline in such alarming proportions that their one prospect is bankruptcy. Already, publications such as *Marie-Claire*, *France-Dimanche*, *Paris-Match*, *Life*, *Reader's Digest*, *Intimité*, and *Stern*, to mention only these, have thrown in the towel. Theaters are closing their doors one after the other. Films crammed with vulgarity, low-grade violence, and dense plots are no longer making money, but are devouring millions in deficits which have the producers baffled. Radio has no listeners, and only the old or sorely overworked still watch TV. On the record market as well, a tradewind is blowing which no one could have forecast. The vocal disappeared in a definitive debacle in 1977, but in 1980 pop and improvised jazz have suddenly hit upon the same doldrums. Suddenly, the rending cries of Lester Young, Charlie Parker, Varèse, Armstrong, Ornette Coleman, Mingus, and Bartók (rediscovered with a certain feverish zeal) are preferred to the monotonous melodies of pop and the interminable lowings of free jazz. But it is literature, still, which evinces the most spectacular reversals. For two or three years now, the books of Sagan, Druon, Kessel, Troyat, Dutourd, Mallet-Joris, Daninos, or any of the best sellers of the 70's, have not sold a single copy. On the other hand, a vast public of indolent and disgusted readers have flocked to the works of heartsick professionals such as Céline, Beckett, Michaux, Sternberg, Bierce, Kafka, Cavanna, Benchley, and above all Cioran, whose *Précis of Decomposition* sold five hundred copies between 1949 and 1975, but enjoyed sales of ten million in 1980, and has established itself as the new Bible of modern times. By the same token, no publisher has managed to market a book on management or marketing, those moth-eaten themes of 1970, or any book of poetry, history, politics, sociology, or metaphysics. These thought-provoking bugbears have finally bored, disgusted, and fatigued the public which still reads. That is to say, the new generation alone. The old lives on, exhausted by daily cares, traffic, the mortal fear of revolution, contributions, timetables, and the agony of leisure. It's an achievement if, when night falls, the old folks have the energy to collapse in front of the TV. In other words, the sales and receipts of intellectual fare, in 1980, reflect only the tastes and preferences of the public from fifteen to thirty-five. The others no longer are consumers of film or books: only of steaks and tranquilizers.

It's the memorable Bastille Day of the Cars, October 10, 1981, that will have marked the declaration of open hostilities that brewed in silent hatred for more than twenty years, between the embattled pedestrians and exasperated drivers.

Prepared in secret, but with meticulous care, the action of October 10th was carried out the same night in all the

great cities of the world, resulting in the systematic destruction by dawn of a hundred million cars. This deliberate (and liberating) massacre-for-revenge left its victims in a dazed stupor of incomprehension. The press
didn't have columns enough to vent its indignation; but
neither did the police have agents enough to arrest the
culprits, who numbered in the millions, and were perfectly organized in their total lack of organization.

From now on, it's war. The two blocs will keep their
hatred fresh and waiting, and nothing will allay their
mutual mistrust. The old generation has just discovered
that the other—coming up without any desire to get on
—is capable of anything, although it was thought to be
merely apathetic. It is, indeed, capable of destroying private property, although it was thought hardly up to chop-
ping down a few trees, and uprooting some public
benches.

With or without the world's approval, the sun of October 11, 1981, rose on a scene in all cities that was rather
remarkable. Fantastic, rather. Few cars were in running
order, and those had to somehow find their way through
the thousands of cranes, bulldozers, and tow trucks that
were removing for disposal in the countryside millions of
cars reduced to scrap. And, to provide the last touch to
this nightmare of property, the insurance companies refused to pay.

The consternation of the consumer on wheels was
matched by the secret satisfaction of the car manufacturers. Business was in danger of becoming very good
that year, since people cannot do without their cars any
more, and will go without eating in order to replace their
little four-wheeled treasures. A satisfaction that ended
abruptly in the shortest possible time. Fifteen days after
the destruction of the cars, a parallel act of sabotage was

carried out everywhere against the factories of the automobile industry, and all their fuel depots.

This time again, in a single night, the factories went
down under an avalanche of steel; the tanks of gas exploded in one great fireworks. Anger was mixed with
growing panic. A panic justified by a new development,
which boded no good for the future: this general, concerted sabotage had been carried out with the support
and participation of all the autoworkers. This might lead
anywhere. If proletarian-pedestrian solidarity is achieved,
the world may well ask itself where it's headed.

For the moment, it's headed wherever it may be *on
foot*, and for some time to come. About a gallon of gas
remains in the world, and that's plenty for whatever cars
are left.

The world is not only going on foot, but is also headed
for the gradual downfall of consumerism. The example
of the sabotage of the automobile industry was followed
in a few months' time by all workers in the chemical,
electronic, and metallurgic industries. A whole world
collapsing in a terrifying uproar of concerted destruction.
A whole other world will henceforward find itself without
radio, TV, immovable steel beams, and detergents. The
press cannot even protest the scandal, the outrage, the
vandalism. The typographers and printing employees have
rallied to the cause of those who rebel and wish to break
this civilization. They have thrown in the wastepaper
basket the vengeful articles handed in for typesetting by
conservative journalists. It is, in fact, the propaganda of
good sense and the satiated middle class. The Caus,
Droits, Dutourds, and Duponts can only keep their traps
shut. The legal rights of the Nourissiers will no longer
nourish them. Discouraged, most of the dailies are tight-
ening their belts and bringing out their last editions. Only

Charlie Hebdo has become a daily, appearing under the provisional title of *France Harakiri*.

How can private enterprise be protected? The entrepreneurs have trouble seeing what exactly they can do. The great magnates would gladly protect their factories and property with cordons of machine guns and artillery, except that they're off the market. The munitions makers closed shop once and for all several years ago, since in 1975 it became impossible to raise an army, or, consequently, start a war. Who, among the young between twenty and thirty, would respond to a call to arms? And to compel the old to man the front is an act which no government has the decency and logic to contemplate.

Light industry and small business are hardly doing better than the great corporations. The old generation is steeped and pickled in its economies, panic stricken at the idea of spending a penny in vain. And the new generation needs nothing, and buys almost nothing. Only the bare essentials. The promoters of fashion and the household arts, of personal property and real estate, are tearing out their hair, eating their balance sheets. Even the drugstores and cafés are going under. That says everything.

After having dismantled the skeleton of the consumer society, the insurgents have dealt it another blow, which removes any chance of its recovering. They are attacking the nerve center of this society: advertising.

In a single day, which in time to come will be called "Anti-Ad Day," everywhere in the world millions of calm rebels have mutilated all the signs, burned the few futilitarian magazines still on the market, and set fire to all the advertising agencies. They now contemplate the burning hearth of this civilization; they fill the streets, sit down in immobile groups along the curbs, clustering into mobs of several thousand silent demonstrators, arrogant, haughty, content with what they have accomplished. Nearly everywhere in the world, governments are losing their *sangfroid*, and dispatching the police or special intervention squads to charge down the streets. Their desire to put down the demonstrators has suffered a setback unique in history, which will prove a fatal blow to repressive regimes. The police, generally young and badly paid enough to openly oppose the capitalist generation, have joined the demonstrators and sat down with them in the streets. That was the end. Without police or an army, how does one repress? Only the property owners, bosses, and businessmen themselves are left to launch an attack on their own behalf, to pay for their cause with their lives. But no fear; they are too cowardly for that. Besides, they have been in the minority for many years now. And from now on, in an overwhelming minority. Whether from fear, conviction, or conversion, millions of men between forty and fifty have taken advantage of these events to leave everything behind them—work, family, business, children, dogs, and furniture—to silently enter the ranks of the destroyers of this civilization, rallying to their cause-without-a-cause. Others, terrified at the idea of losing their goods and their businesses, have opted for suicide. Still others have fled with their bank accounts to Switzerland, one of the few countries where nothing has happened yet, where nothing ever will happen. But, in one way or another, the Armageddon of consumerism is underway, and one cannot see how the kingpins of commerce can possibly win.

A fact also unique in history: this enormous, perfectly coordinated mass movement hardly seems to care about anything, not even the formation of a single well-defined party, or the organization of a summit meeting, or the election of leaders, or *even* an ultimate split into numberless dissident and loquacious little groups. Millions of human beings are acting with one accord, like an enormous octopus whose hundreds of tentacles move all in the same manner, doing the same thing for one purpose. A goal which is none other than that of never having any goal again. One ideal that has no ideal. Everywhere, the dull resonance of the word "nothing" holds sway over the heart of the community at large; the general awareness is directed only towards an imperative need to renounce. A renunciation which not only has resulted in rampages, fires, and explosions, but which has created experts. What, for so long, the right as well as the left found so difficult to obtain, despite torrents of abuse, promises, harangues, slogans, and shouting, the party of indolence has come by without effort: partisans! And this without holding meetings, raising banners, distributing pamphlets, or performing oratory. Everywhere, at every moment, painters are throwing down their brushes, actors foresaking the termite-infested boards, writers their typewriters; acting attorneys are walking out on their barbecues and their responsibilities, employees are abandoning their limited ambitions, and uncounted underlings are quitting without bothering to give notice.

And to prove in the sight of heaven that there is no longer any enduring faith, no more myths to refurbish, or religious ornaments to take down, in March 1983 the first churches were put to the torch; others soon followed. The pope committed suicide a few days later, an act which was received with the most profound indifference. Only one cardinal followed his master in death, again with the same indifference.

From this year on, there regularly occurred resignations, or more often flights, of heads of State, ministers, or other politicians condemned to high office. Again, these events took place accompanied by the most uncompromising indifference. Formerly, it was hatred and envy that emanated from the opposition towards those in power; now, it is no more than icy disdain. For years now, certain high-ranking reactionaries have tried to redress the situation by means of speeches, promises, and imprecations. In vain: their acts are invariably received with ridicule. Their words convince only those who are slowly but inevitably going downhill: the old, the painstaking, the friends of order and the Bank Account, of schedules and efficiency. The others, who were supposed to take the baton, no longer even listen. Nothing happens, nothing moves. The world is slowly being transformed into a huge boulder: a few kicks won't set it rolling.

This is the reason why, since 1980, no one has dared suggest a vote, a referendum, or a cabinet ouster. They are well aware that no one would go to the trouble of voting. Or else, a huge majority would vote "no vote." Or vote *against* everything without bothering to think. The muck of politics interests no one any more; no one wants to even get their toes wet, or hear any talk of it. Governments prefer to pass it over, and pretend that the problem doesn't exist. The less conspicuous the authorities, the safer they are. And for the moment, miraculously, no one is talking about his salary. No one's worrying about that, any more than they worry about the dividend millionaires or company presidents who are quite often deprived of almost their entire staff. At any rate, "personnel" as such hardly exists any more. The frailer employees are dying off, in a rhythm accelerated by the absence of young doctors to take over from the old doctors who, one after the other, are going off to the graveyard to tend the zombies. The more farsighted ones have fled to Switzerland, Bermuda, or Alaska, the few nooks and crannies of the world that persist unchanged. There they are still trembling over their narrow escape. A needless terror, besides, for the revolution which has completely reversed the social order has been accomplished without bloodshed, coercion, victims, machine-gun bursts, or incarceration. With one accord, nonviolence has been established as the norm, and is observed to the letter. There is destruction, perhaps; but it is polite, and calmly executed. There's not even shouting in the streets. The attack is on institutions, things, and facades: never on the living.

In the same way, for ten years now, among the formidable mass of professionally unemployed who no longer wish to *spend* their lives under pretext of *earning* them, solidarity has been total, a foregone conclusion, normal, never faulted. It has become a state of affairs as usual as the former avarice, egotism, and lust for property. Those who have rich relations or parents well off, private incomes, or secret sources of cash support the others, very often putting them up in the city, or in their villas or country houses. They give them money to live on, knowing that the idea of superfluous wealth is ever less seductive, and just about dead. Those unemployed have few needs and few desires, certainly not those of accumulating property, or encumbering themselves with useless objects. They possess almost nothing, and are not particularly attached to what they do possess. They willingly leave the cities for the country, where life is easier, especially the seashore. In France alone, the number of disgusted citizens who have quietly colonized the Côte d'Azur, and the vast, deserted beaches of the Atlantic, is estimated at ten million. The Parisian region must now have only some five million inhabitants.

What the ambitious moneyed class dreads most is theft and looting in private enterprise. It lives panic stricken by this obsession. But the nonworkers have stolen nothing. They simply demand, calmly, what they have need of. And they are given it in abundance by the others, who are glad to get off so easily. Never have parents been so generous with their children, never have the rich supported so many disinherited black sheep.

Nevertheless, in 1985, the Fatigued Generation—such is the name instantaneously devised for it—strong with the force of accumulated inertia, and the nervous apathy of the older generation, attempted a *coup d'état* which indeed seemed to sound the knell of an ancestral reign: that of legalized and governmentalized swindling. It had to do with the Contributions system, left intact, but with an altered purpose. Henceforth, the revenues coming from those with money would go, not into the Public Treasury, but directly to the *Public:* i.e. to the millions of people who were no longer working because they refused to participate in the general neurosis. It was an incredible reversal which changed everything around. The money of drudges and their exploiters would finally be used, not to pay for bribes, police, rockets, guns, state banquets, or highways, but to provide wine and bread to those without. The revolutionists in no way abused their power to profit from the situation by increasing taxes. They left them at the former rates. This was because, on the one hand, they didn't wish to be bothered with a complex reorganization, and on the other, because the current income was sufficient. They had no more wish to accumulate income than they had to work: survival itself seemed to them an occupation like any other, difficult, essential and more important, even, than hanging out the laundry, or airing the files. They truly desired nothing else, and had no other claims to press.

Furthermore, concerning the matter of taxes, they had complete confidence in the old treasury methods of extracting payment in the shortest possible time. But money for their survival they did not spend in purchases liable to encourage business, which was dying out almost everywhere. They made no useless purchases that would return the money they had gotten from the merchants to begin with. They used the money to get away, to settle as far away as possible from any trace of civilization.

A year later, the Parisian revolutionists cracked down on the lottery, the average Frenchman's favorite way of losing money. Paris had been nothing but a lottery for too long, in fact. This afforded the new beneficiaries a regular and sizable income. This truly signaled the end, and the beginning of something else. In the U.S., the same kind of revolutionists did away with underworld regimes—the prostitution monopolies and such like of the Mafia. Consternation was mingled with panic. If the recognized gangsters of the world were being robbed, where was the world heading? Towards what anarchy?

For the first time, a man of the new generation is attempting to take power. He is trying to arouse the electorate with statements of principle, watchwords, and exciting slogans. His ethic is plainly different from the traditional ones, but his solemn tone evokes that of all politicians. His principal theories are simple and short, accompanied by equally terse corollaries. "The only future of man is death. Nothing is worth doing because we all die. Nothing is of any use, not even the word 'nothing.' Useless to earn money, because, in so doing, one irretrievably wastes one's life. Man cannot be a property owner, since he is no more than the tenant of his own body. To build a future for himself means only to construct his own tomb. This planet is nothing but a cemetery: why furnish it? The one logical task that a man can undertake is that of survival: the rest is a mirage." And so on.

His phrases and his arguments drop from his lips into oblivion. What he says, the whole world thinks and knows for a fact. No one needs a loudspeaker to shout out precepts that everyone is applying to the letter without orders from anyone. This noisy, loud-mouthed, shifty orator is judged above all with contempt. To take the trouble of mounting the podium to denounce ambition can only be an act of ambition. To speak of the absurd is no less absurd. After a few weeks, having picked up no partisans or listeners, he withdraws. Forever. No possible doubt about it: for the first time, the world has changed because man himself has changed.

But if the phrase has perished in the periphrase, and the discourse has finally run its course, as it seems, the day of the coldly executed act is in its prime. Nor do we mean purposeless acts, or minor measures taken on the sly to save face and protect major interests, but precise acts that question a whole way of life.

The most spectacular of such acts must indeed have been the abolition, in 1989, of rents. It was decided that professional landlords had nothing coming to them, that the right to a roof over one's head was as normal as one's right to the sky and the beach ball, to the sun's rays and the sandbox. Just as the dead are entitled to their grave without having to pay rent on it. Yet another measure, revolutionary of course, but proving that this *fin-de-siècle*

world was curiously reducing its aims, haunted, it seems,
by a certain spirit of black humor, as well as a clearly defined will to bring everything back to the essential, was
the removal of financial constraints and little, niggling
compensations. Death and life became the sole obses-
sions of a whole new race. And since, while waiting for
death, one had to live, advantage was taken of the last
spasms of the communications world to take a census of
all empty premises, which were officially occupied without asking the owner's leave. This might have made for
trouble, a last gasp of the reactionaries; but nothing happened. The reactionaries have run out of reactions. Above
all, they have no arms, army, or police. They've capitulated in dismay, abandoned their rights one after the
other, as the sea abandons the sand at low tide. They are
silent, overwhelmed, and are waiting only for the end,
and a decent burial in the family vault. They believe, as
by intuition, that surely this right will be granted them
without argument. There's one shadow in the picture:
they are in danger of earning this right only after having
lost all the others. And yet there's a compensation: they
will die without ever having understood what befell them,
done in not by heaven, but simply by those on Earth. No
need to mention that, for years now, the mortality rate
among the propertied classes has been shocking. Worries
about money, egocentric anxieties, banking dramas, and
concerns about the safe-deposit box are decimating them
as much as, if not more than, the pollution of yesteryear.

We are approaching the much advertised year 2000,
but the century's in danger of arriving there in bad shape.
Having lost all its ostentation en route. It is in the United
States that the fatal blow will have been dealt a prosper-
ous and very old industry: that of the food trades.

A group of old agronomists, who have been living in California for ten years, manage, by dint of very complex graftings and tentative experiments, to grow a sort of dwarf shrub which yields enormous fruits. Fruits whose taste is somewhere between hearts of palm, steak tartar, and caviar. Not only does their flesh contain all the vitamins, but it is refreshing, and has latent euphoric properties, exactly like alcohol or marihuana. With the difference that these fruits do not at all endanger health. And their nutritive values are astonishing. A few fruits a day suffice to nourish the normal individual.

This miracle food arrived in Europe, where a gourmet was heard to cry: "I would swear I was at the Vefour!" an allusion to one of the holy places of cuisine, long since gone under in the collapse of starred eating establishments. The phrase bore fruit. Throughout the world the providentially discovered fruit came to be called the "vefour," and was henceforward planted as formerly the potato, wheat, and rice had been. A detail not to be ignored was that the vefour grows without care, without work, and fast as hell, anywhere. It shoots up in the sand of deserts, as well as in the rocky terrain of mountains. A whole generation of indolent nomads without ambition would henceforth feed on the vefour. With lodging and food free, their survival was assured. On the other hand, the death of the food trades was equally assured. Bakers, innkeepers, butchers, grocers, and dairy-store owners, all such little folk, the pride and glory of the thick-witted bourgeoisie, went bankrupt right away. A shameful bankruptcy, which there was no one to regret.

This quiet food revolution brought to a neat end the apogee of great cities and menial jobs, which one had to put up with, or starve to death. From 1995 on, waves of disgusted citizens, unleashed from the cities, emigrated to the wind and sun, relaxation and rain, seashores and mountains. In the cities, especially the capitals, the farce was concluded. The sure values were the ones that went down the most surely; the jobs with a future belonged to a past gone by; promotion had lost its means of locomotion, all the firms were infirm, major undertakings seemed to be secretly managed by actual undertakers and, all in all, it seemed better, for survival's sake, to go off and plant the vefour somewhere, than to consider such outmoded occupations as those of hairdresser, cabinet minister, industrialist, fireman, decorator, publicist, or movie star.

In other words, the year 2000 for which history has been waiting for so long, and with such emotion, will dawn upon a spectacle the likes of which no one would have dared imagine.

Industry no longer exists, commerce belongs to the past, politics and government have been discarded, and declared to be of no public use, the fine arts are completely stagnant, and official institutions have been officially junked. Real estate belongs to the same unreal past, banks have gone bankrupt, and generally, the civilization of a century drunk with progress, consumerism, benefits, and business is to be summed up in the profit and loss columns.

There are no more airplanes in the sky, trains on the rails, cars on the highways, machines in the factories, elevators in the buildings. They've cut the engines of the planet; there's no electricity in the wires, not a drop of gas in the storage tanks. A whole class made cripples by the automobile has found its legs, for walking or pedaling. The era of speed has passed, which bothers no one, because no one ever thinks of saving time any more. There are no more matters of importance to settle at the ends of the world, no product that has to be delivered by express service. No one thinks of traveling any more. The "Jet Set" society has vanished in the ridicule which it inspired. Man has finally understood that nothing resembles a beach more than another beach, and that there's no point in traveling six thousand miles for the sunshine which one can find anywhere.

On the seas and rivers, one goes by sail, just as on the roads one rides a bicycle. The waters swarm with navigators, and have, ever since the exodus to nature. Many live on sailboats which they have built themselves, and thrive on fish, sun, gusts of wind, and the intoxication of the helm. As for those who don't have sea legs, and can't stand solitude, they live in communities of fifty to a hundred people, rarely more. They live on fruits, vegetables, and above all the vefour, and are nearly always vegetarians. Just as they have rejected firearms, they never hunt, and have not been ridiculous enough to rediscover the bow and arrow or the arbalest.

They've swept the big cities clean of the vestiges of the past, including those which might have had some interest for them. Most of their communities have communal libraries, record and even film libraries, which can only contain works done before 1985, when all systematic production ceased. But for all that, the arts aren't dead. They have simply become those of the artisan. There are writers who type out their novels, and circulate them in manuscript. Painters exhibit their works without thought of sales. Sculptors decorate nature with their sculptures. Musicians play out their inspiration to no audience.

Money is no longer current, and is worth nothing because nothing is for sale. Barter has replaced it, according to supply and demand. Man having lost his instincts of rapacity and ambition, there are no criminals. No one steals; there are no crimes, not even sexual crimes or crimes of passion. Sexual liberty is of course total; marriage has been abolished, and "to have a woman" is an old-hat turn of phrase which makes everyone who hears it smile. Anyway, it is not passion that holds sway in the bosom of the communities, but rather tenderness. The vefour, in fact, has proven to be a fruit that inspires neither savage appetites nor lewdness, acting, instead, as a tranquilizer, or, more exactly, a soother.

How many years have passed thus? Hard to say, for since the opening years of the twenty-first century, we have lost all sense of the calendar, of months, and days, just as we've lost the sense of schedules and even of time.

Whereas life formerly went on in neurosis and frenzy, murderous fury and the lust for gain, now it unfolds in calm and leisure, indolence and wisdom.

The Fatigued Generation now calls itself the Zero Generation. The old, used up, decimated, ulcer ridden, have disappeared. There remain from it only a few survivors who are willingly provided with what they need, it being thought that one owes them at least that. The population of the earth is declining as well, since the Zero Generation has very few children. It does not feel, in any profound way, the need to procreate. It has become lucid and unsentimental, rid of all Christian or Maoist prejudices, well off without its fetishes and moralizing proverbs, cold to all ideals, but aware of the end before any desire; it no longer believes in the absolute necessity of repeopling the planet, any more than it does in refurnishing it. In other words, the headlong river of the centuries seems to have suddenly emptied into a lake of time, a dead lake, stagnant, where it is pleasant to float under water, in silence, calmly, in an atmosphere of vacations, of vague vacuity, peace, pacifism and ironic indifference.

Such was the state of affairs when, from another galaxy, the Druges landed on earth.

In force. There were more than a million of them. They had for a long time envisaged the colonization of this planet of secondary importance, and the moment seemed well chosen to them for carrying out their mission.

The Druges might have disappointed lovers of the unusual. They did not have wings like vultures, or plates like lobsters, or even fins like pikes; they didn't spit fire, or wave tentacles; nor did they get about on six webbed feet. They resembled us like brothers. Same eyes, same nose in the middle of the face, above a mouth out of which nothing came but words; same size, same corpulence. They even possessed that smile—so gentle—which had been our glory.

The Earthlings, who had long ago lost any idea of racism, welcomed them with full simplicity and warmth.

"Welcome! Peace! Love!" intoned the Californians who were the first to encounter the Druges.

At these words, the Druges opened fire.

It was the signal for the massacre. A memorable massacre, in which all but a few Earthlings perished.

The Druges did, in fact, resemble the Earthlings like brothers. But those of the 1950's.